Sammy Skunk's Super Sniffer

by Barbara deRubertis • illustrated by R.W. Alley

THE KANE PRESS / NEW YORK

Alpha Betty's Class

Alexander Anteater

Bobby Baboon

Corky Cub

Dilly Dog

Eddie Elephant

Frances Frog

Gertie Gorilla

Hanna Hippo

Izzy Impala

Jeremy Jackrabbit

Kylie Kangaroo

Lana Llama

Maxwell Moose

Nina Nandu

Oliver Otter

Polly Porcupine

Quentin Quokka

STAR of the BOOK

Rosie Raccoon

Sammy Skunk

Tessa Tiger

Umma Ungka

Victor Vicuna

Walter Warthog

Xavier Ox

Yoko Yak

Zachary Zebra

Alpha Betty

Library of Congress Cataloging-in-Publication Data

deRubertis, Barbara.
Sammy Skunk's super sniffer / by Barbara deRubertis ; illustrated by R.W. Alley.
p. cm. — (Animal antics A to Z)
Summary: Sammy Skunk uses his amazing sense of smell and his cooking skills
to help the new school cook.
ISBN 978-1-57565-352-5 (library binding : alk. paper) — ISBN 978-1-57565-344-0
(pbk. : alk. paper) — ISBN 978-1-57565-383-9 (e-book)
[1. Smell—Fiction. 2. Senses and sensation—Fiction. 3. Skunks—Fiction. 4. Animals—Fiction.
5. Alphabet. 6. Humorous stories.] I. Alley, R. W. (Robert W.) ill. II. Title.
PZ7.D4475Sam 2011
[E]—dc22   2010051307

1 3 5 7 9 10 8 6 4 2

First published in the United States of America in 2011 by Kane Press, Inc.
Printed in the United States of America
WOZ0711

Series Editor: Juliana Hanford
Book Design: Edward Miller

Animal Antics A to Z is a registered trademark of Kane Press, Inc.

www.kanepress.com

Even when Sammy Skunk was just a little stinker, he had a super sniffer.

He liked to help his parents cook squash soup.
Sammy would sit on Papa's shoulders.
And Papa would stir the simmering soup.

"Sam, my man! What do you think?"
Papa would say.

Sammy would sniff. And sniff.

Sometimes Sammy smiled.
Mama and Papa knew what that meant.
The soup was good!

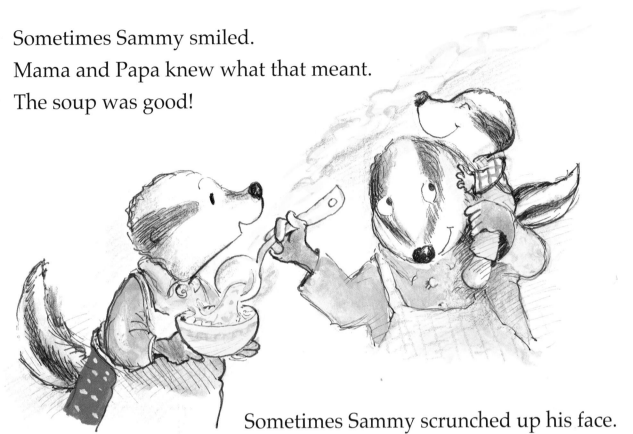

Sometimes Sammy scrunched up his face.
Mama and Papa knew what that meant, too!

"Oh, Sammykins!" Mama would say.
"What does the soup need?"
Then Sammy would point to something.
And Mama would sprinkle it in the pot.

Soon Sammy was an honest-to-goodness
soup expert!

Before Sammy started school, his parents told his teacher all about his super sniffer.

"How useful!" said his teacher, Alpha Betty.

At recess on the first day, Sammy put
his sniffer to work.
"Don't step there!" he called out.
And he pointed to some inky, stinky mud.

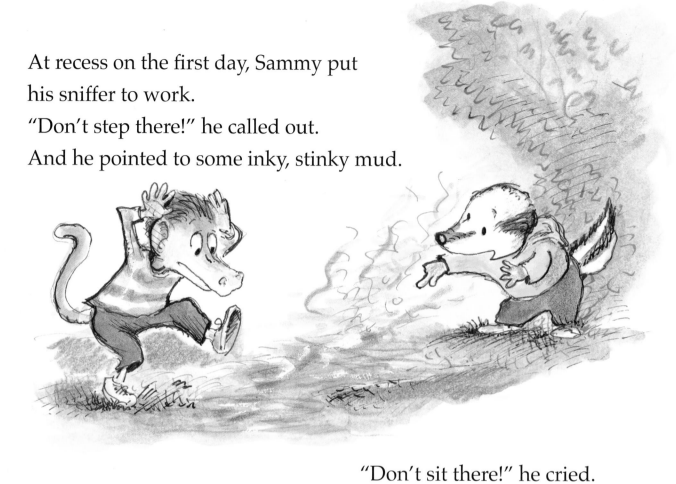

"Don't sit there!" he cried.
And he pointed to some icky,
sticky sap.

But when it was time for lunch, Sammy's
super sniffer caused a problem!

Alpha Betty led her class to the lunch room.
"Students, I'd like you to meet Susie Horse.
Susie is our new school cook.
She'll be fixing tasty soups for our lunches."

Susie served bowls of soup to everyone.

Sammy sniffed his soup.

He squinted his eyes.

He scrunched up his nose.

And he whispered, "Don't eat the soup!"

Susie Horse was NOT pleased.

"Is there a *problem* with my soup?"
she asked Sammy.

"I'm sorry, Susie," Sammy said.
He took a small sip of his soup.
Then he set down his spoon.
"I guess I'm just not hungry," he said.

No one else seemed hungry either.
Susie scowled.

The next day Susie served a different soup.
All the students watched Sammy.

He sniffed.
He squinted his eyes.
He scrunched up his nose.
And he tried to swallow a BIG spoonful of soup.

Suddenly Sammy *SNEEZED! A-SHOO!*

Soup spurted out of his mouth and his nose!

"I'm SO sorry, Susie," said Sammy.
He wiped up the soupy mess.
Susie was silent as a stone.
And her face was stormy!

Alpha Betty tried to explain about Sammy's sniffer.
Susie Horse still scowled. "Then let Mr. Super
Sniffer fix the soup," she said.

Alpha Betty smiled.
"Would you like to try, Sammy?" she asked.

"Sure," said Sammy. "If it's okay with Susie."

Susie's face still looked stormy.
"Okay, Mr. Super Sniffer," she said.
"Come back tomorrow morning during recess."

When Alpha Betty took Sammy to the kitchen
the next morning, he was shaking in his boots.

Susie's face was stormier than ever.

"Here's today's soup," Susie said.
She pointed to a steaming pot.

"What kind of soup is it?" Sammy asked.

"It's squash soup," said Susie.
"It's made with squash. And water."

"Oh!" said Sammy. "Sometimes I help my
parents make squash soup!
We add lots of stuff to make it super tasty."

Susie squinted her eyes.
"What sort of 'stuff'?" she asked.

"I'll show you!" said Sammy.
He scooped up carrots. Celery.
Onions. And apples!

Susie fussed as she sliced and diced.
"Apples in squash soup?
I've never heard of such a thing."

But Sammy was just getting started.

He said, "Shake in some of this and that.
Sprinkle in some of these and those.
Now smush it all together!"

Susie scowled as she smushed.

"This isn't squash soup," she snapped.

"This is a big, sloppy MESS."

Sammy took a looong, slooow sniff.

And he smiled a BIG smile.

"Taste it, Susie!" said Sammy.

Susie looked disgusted.
But she took a tiny sip.

She didn't smile.
But she didn't scowl either.

Then she slurped up a large spoonful.
The corners of her mouth twitched.
And slowly, Susie smiled a tiny little smile.

"Morning recess is over, Susie," said Sammy.
"I'll see you at lunch!"

Susie stared. Then she whispered,
"Thanks, Sammy."

At lunch, Susie served big bowls of squash soup.

Everyone's eyes were on Sammy.
He sniffed. He tasted.
And he smiled a BIG smile.

Today *everyone* was hungry!
No one talked. The only sound in the
lunch room was *slurping*!

Alpha Betty whispered in Susie's ear.
"The soup is simply delicious!"

Susie sat down next to Sammy Skunk.
"Will you bring your super sniffer to help
me tomorrow, Sammy?" she asked.

"Sure!" said Sammy.

And Susie smiled her BIGGEST smile.

Then everyone had a second helping of the best
squash soup EVER!

Even Susie Horse!

STAR OF THE BOOK: THE SKUNK

FUN FACTS

- **Home:** Skunks live in North and South America and on some islands in Asia. They can dig their own holes for shelter . . . or live in hollow logs, rock piles, or even junk piles.
- **Appearance:** All skunks are striped, but there are many different patterns of stripes. Some skunks even have spots!
- **Food:** Skunks eat many different plants, insects, and small animals. They are also attracted to humans' garbage!
- **Did You Know?** Of course, skunks are best known for the VERY stinky liquid they spray when they are in danger. But *part* of this liquid has been used in making perfume!

LOOK BACK

Learning to identify letter sounds (phonemes) at the beginning, middle, and end of words is called "phonemic awareness."

- The word *soup* <u>starts</u> with the *s* sound. Listen to the words on page 22 being read again. When you hear a word that <u>starts</u> with the *s* sound, stand up and say "____ <u>starts</u> with *sss*!"
- The word *mess* <u>ends</u> with the *s* sound. Listen to the words on page 11 being read again. When you hear a word that <u>ends</u> with the *s* sound, stand up and say "____ <u>ends</u> with *sss*!"
- **Challenge:** The word *last* begins with the *l* sound and ends with the *s-t* sounds. Change the *l* to *f* and make a word that rhymes with *last*. Now change the *f* to *p* and make another word that rhymes with *last*.

TRY THIS!

Stand up and listen carefully as each word in the word bank below is read aloud slowly.

- If the word <u>begins</u> with the *s* sound, put your hands on your head!
- If the word has the *s* sound in the <u>middle</u>, put your hands on your tummy!
- If the word <u>ends</u> with the *s* sound, put your hands on your feet!

> skunk horse castle soup whisper
> hips useful sneeze guess sniff mess
> tasty stir boots fussing smile

FOR MORE ACTIVITIES, go to Sammy Skunk's website: www.kanepress.com/AnimalAntics/SammySkunk.html
You'll also find a recipe for Sammy Skunk's Squash Soup!

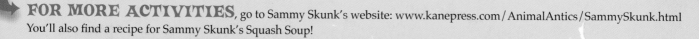

Managing
Brand
YOU

Managing
Brand
YOU

SEVEN STEPS TO CREATING
YOUR MOST SUCCESSFUL SELF

JERRY S. WILSON

and

IRA BLUMENTHAL

⁂AMACOM

American Management Association
New York • Atlanta • Brussels • Chicago • Mexico City • San Francisco
Shanghai • Tokyo • Toronto • Washington, D.C.

Special discounts on bulk quantities of AMACOM books are
available to corporations, professional associations, and other
organizations. For details, contact Special Sales Department,
AMACOM, a division of American Management Association,
1601 Broadway, New York, NY 10019.
Tel.: 212-903-8316.   Fax: 212-903-8083.
Website: www.amacombooks.org/go/specialsales

This publication is designed to provide accurate and authoritative
information in regard to the subject matter covered. It is sold with the
understanding that the publisher is not engaged in rendering legal,
accounting, or other professional service. If legal advice or other expert
assistance is required, the services of a competent professional person
should be sought.

Library of Congress Cataloging-in-Publication Data

Wilson, Jerry S.
  Managing brand you : seven steps to creating your most successful self /
Jerry S. Wilson and Ira Blumenthal.
      p.   cm.
    Includes bibliographical references and index.
    ISBN-13: 978-0-8144-1068-4
    ISBN-10: 0-8144-1068-5
    1. Success.   2. Branding (Marketing)   I. Blumenthal, Ira.   II. Title.

  BF637.S8W526   2008
  650.1—dc22
                                                                2007051366

Printing number

10   9   8   7   6   5   4   3   2   1

From Jerry S. Wilson:

To
My wife Ginny and our daughter Abby,
my best friends and personal inspiration

From Ira Blumenthal:

For Sharon, Julie, John, Jonathan, Eric, Jeffrey, Ryan and
most especially, most importantly, most affectionately,
most lovingly . . . for Kim

Contents

Contents

ACKNOWLEDGMENTS

FROM JERRY S. WILSON

Over the past several years, *Managing Brand YOU* has been a personal passion of mine that has evolved with the help of many people. From speech to speech and seminar to seminar, over 2,000 people have put their fingerprint on this 7 Step System for self-development by providing their feedback and support.

These sessions have proven that there is a huge population of people committed to improving their personal situation, have the desire to develop, and are searching for a personal roadmap to make their desires a reality. Hopefully, *Managing Brand YOU* fulfills this desire. If this book inspires one person to greater fulfillment, it will have been a worthy effort.

There are so many people who contributed to this labor of love, but several people stand out. While I have dedicated this book to my wife Virginia and our daughter Abigail, I must begin with my personal acknowledgment of how much their love and affection has lifted my life. Not only did they encourage me to put this concept on paper, but they also contributed with content, late night proofreading, and the ultimate picture of success. For this, I am eternally grateful.

Certainly, I must thank our agent, Loretta Barrett, for her representation that led us to the ideal publishing group of AMACOM. Our senior editor, Jacqueline Flynn; associate editor,

Mike Sivilli; and their capable team have been a pleasure to work with throughout this journey.

I must thank my mother, Helen, and father, Jerry, for instilling in me a set of values that has driven me throughout my life. Both of them provided the environment for my sister, Mary, and brother, Tom, to understand what is right and wrong, and take accountability for our actions in life.

I am blessed to have spent two decades thriving in a corporate culture founded on refreshment and moments of enjoyment, The Coca-Cola Company. I must single out a few very special Coca-Cola people who have fully endorsed my development of this body of work while "doing my day job" of leading a global business unit. E. Neville Isdell, Chairman of the Board, my previous manager and mentor, never blinked an eye when I first asked for his advice and authorization to write this book. He has encouraged me all along the way, and I consider him a true friend and motivational leader. Muhtar Kent, CEO and my direct manager, has provided his unwavering support and positive reinforcement to make this concept a reality. Cynthia McCague, Senior Vice President and Director of Human Resources, has been a constant source of energy and excitement all along the way. Geoffrey Kelly, General Counsel, has been a great corporate steward, advisor, and student of the *Managing Brand YOU* idea. Ceree Eberly, Group Human Resource Director for the European Union, and a great friend, worked with me during the developmental years while providing personal strength. Caroline Jackson, Chief Human Resource Officer for North America, has been a dear friend for many years, and continues to be a source of pride, integrity, and passion. I greatly appreciate Daphne Schechter and Jeff Halter who both identified early on the potential of this idea, and challenged my

thinking along the way. I also want to thank my entire global team who represents the principles embedded in *Managing Brand YOU*, especially Melinda Tinsley, my administrator, and Rich DeAugustinis, my executive assistant. Both Melinda and Rich have stood side by side with me while I managed the reality of a global business with my "weekend and late night" endeavor of this journey called *Managing Brand YOU*.

Over the past few years I have referenced my desire to take *Managing Brand YOU* from an interesting speech to a complete guide in the form of a book many times. Yet, this vision had never materialized. Coincidentally, one day, in the office corridors, I reconnected with my friend of 18 years, Ira Blumenthal, who shared my brand beliefs. In the course of a ten-minute conversation, we agreed to make this dream a collective reality. Ira brought his existing talents in the publishing world, and through his hard work we have a top agent, world-class publisher, and a completed work to be very proud of. I am very grateful to Ira for helping a dream of mine become a reality.

Finally, I would like to acknowledge YOU. Every individual has the potential to be great, and you have taken a symbolic step by purchasing and embracing this book. Only time will tell if you find the success that life has to offer. Many people, just like you, have bought books with the intent of developing themselves. This system is a self-guided and self-monitored approach, leveraging some of the best techniques found in world-class consumer brand companies. It can work if you believe in yourself and take the time to find your very own space of fulfillment.

I thank you for your interest in *Managing Brand YOU*, and invite you to visit our website at www.managingbrandyou.com for further tips and insights.

FROM IRA BLUMENTHAL

Brand Ira is most thankful and appreciative for having an incredibly committed, dedicated, hard working, intuitive, cerebral, visionary co-author in Jerry S. Wilson. Great partnerships are made up of individuals who "fit" and who have complementary skill sets and core competencies. Ours is a great partnership . . . and for that, I'm most grateful. I'd also like to thank my wife, as well as business partner, Kim, who is my inspiration and my rock. She is the wind beneath my wings and is my all time favorite brand.

Managing
Brand
YOU

INTRODUCTION: WHAT BRANDING CAN DO FOR YOU

"If you want to predict the future, create it."
—PETER F. DRUCKER

WHAT DO SUCCESSFUL CONSUMER-GOODS companies know that could help transform your life? And how can you use this knowledge to become a more fulfilled person? The answers to these questions lie in the discipline of building strong brands. What if you could take a page right out of the corporate book of business development and use it to craft and implement dramatic, important changes in yourself that are focused on development of your own life? Successful brands convey a consistent message and create an emotional bond with consumers. Don't we all want to convey a consistent message and create a similar emotional bond with those important people around us? Absolutely! The process of building such brands is widely used in the commercial world, and now you, too, can use these techniques to build a brand-new you—a Brand YOU!

WHAT IF YOU THOUGHT OF YOURSELF AS A BRAND?

Who am I? What do I stand for? What do I *want* to stand for? These are questions that have been asked by people for ages. In our fast-paced, highly competitive, stressful, often chaotic world, it is even more difficult to know what you stand for—what uniqueness you have to offer. Don't stress about this any longer. There is an answer to these deep questions, and the answer comes in the form of the threshold question, What if you thought of yourself as a brand?

What if you not only think of yourself as a brand but also actively analyze your personal brand assets and deficits, and you dedicate yourself to changing or refining Brand YOU? Yes, as strange as it seems, you can dramatically change and grow your life by studying the time-tested precepts, postulates, discipline, and processes of corporate and product branding, and applying them to your personal life. This step can lead to your living the life you've always imagined for yourself.

In the wonderful Christmas movie *Miracle on 34th Street*, Kris Kringle tells a disbelieving child that dreaming of magical holiday moments and a better tomorrow is important. He says, "To me, the imagination is a place all by itself . . . a separate country. Now you've heard of the French nation, the British nation . . . well, this is the Imagi-nation. It's a wonderful place." It's time for you to now book passage on a trip to the magical, mystical "land of imagination." Building a Brand YOU requires that you dig deep into your imagination and visualize what you want to stand for and what spaces in life and business you want to occupy.

So, what if you thought of yourself as a brand? Just imagine, for a moment, that you are, in fact, a brand. Step outside yourself

and look at *you*, your background, your lifestyle, your philosophy of life, and your views on right and wrong, as well as the expressions you use, the stores you frequent, the foods you eat, the clothes you wear. Think of your educational background, your experiences, your special areas of expertise. Consider the features that others respect about you, the features of people you respect and why. These are your personal brand attributes. And now you've made the first move toward establishing your Brand YOU.

BUILDING A NEW BRAND YOU

Yes, you can create your future. It's in your hands. If you commit to the Brand YOU process, you can and *will* succeed. It will take work. It will take focus. It will take time. And in the end, it will all be worth it. In the words of the poet Spirella, "There's no thrill in easy sailing . . . but there is satisfaction that's mighty sweet to take, when you reach a destination that you thought you'd never make."

Why is personal branding so important to you? You may be someone who doesn't believe in "tooting your own horn"—or drawing attention to the things you've done, or do, or plan on doing. You may also believe that if you just do the best you can, good things will automatically come to you. Well, this may be the case for a few lucky individuals, but the majority of people are confused about how they can, in fact, stand out in a crowd, how they can succeed, how they can clearly stand for something, and how they can gain the respect of others. After all, there are times in all of our lives when we'd like to be noticed, to be appreciated for our

personal strengths, competencies, good nature, and insight. Everybody wants to be special and receive respect, acknowledgment, and even admiration from others. The reality is that each of us, regardless of our position in life, wants to be special, hopes to be noticed, craves attention from others, desires respect, and regularly wants to feel important. Who doesn't want to feel (and be) important? And who doesn't want to make a mark on the world we live in, to truly make a difference to the people around us? It's human nature to want to make a difference, whether it's to your family, your significant other, your children, your friends, your business, your community, your house of worship.

Who doesn't want to feel (and be) important? And who doesn't want to leave a mark on the world we live in and truly make a difference to those around us?

Personal branding is relevant to anyone who wants to unleash his or her inner passions and proactively build a fulfilling future, as well as grow in importance, relevance, and reputation. Too many people are just floating down the river of life, expecting that everything will work out in the long run. But why settle for the possibility of life's taking care of itself when you can draw the roadmap that captures the kind of life you envision for yourself? Why not create your own future? It's cute, it's funny, and certainly it's an example that reinforces what we've all known throughout our lives. Too many times in our lives we seem to be waiting for something to just pour into our mouths or fall into our hands—or

for challenges to just work themselves out in the nick of time. But life isn't like that. When changes and challenges confront us, doing nothing will result in—nothing. Business guru and author Price Pritchett wrote, "More of the same gives you one thing . . . more of the same!"

We have to become more proactive, more energetic, more spirited, and more focused on making positive changes in our lives. After all, there are only three things a person can do when confronted with change. Ignore it. React to it. Make other changes. Now, ignoring it will lead to disaster. Did you ever have a toothache? What happens if you ignore that biological change in your mouth? It doesn't get better; it gets worse. The second strategy, reacting to change, will keep a person at status quo and he or she will survive. But is just surviving enough? Of course not. You want to thrive. You want to succeed, to achieve.

Then there's the final strategy in dealing with change: making other changes. Yes, you want to be a catalyst for change—a change agent, as business consultant Peter Drucker has said—to create your future. One theme throughout this book is simply stated as "If it's to be, it's up to me!" Being proactive, being committed to building your personal brand, will allow you to:

> ➤ Identify your inner passions and core essence.
> ➤ Stand up for what is important to you and stand out in the crowd.
> ➤ Focus your energy on meeting your top priorities.
> ➤ Stop spending time doing things that do not excite you.
> ➤ Execute your own personal Brand YOU plan.
> ➤ Achieve fulfillment, personal success, and, ultimately, happiness.

---

*There are only three things you can do when
confronted with change. You can ignore it.
You can react to it. You can make other changes.*

GREAT BRANDS ARE NO ACCIDENT

There's a future for those who plan for it. Great buildings come about as a result of someone's grand vision, then an impressive schematic, a well–thought-out design, a focused layout and structure, and certainly a sound plan with blueprints. Great success in business and in life is typically the result of sound reasoning and stellar planning. Great achievements are no accident. Great success is no accident. Likewise, great brands are no accident. They grow and prosper by plan and planning.

The Coca-Cola Company has a proven history of developing brands that can connect with over 1 billion consumers every day by way of the preeminent beverage-distribution system in the world. It has also built global production and quality control systems that ensure every bottle, can, or cup delivers reliable and enjoyable refreshment to consumers. Coke, like other stellar brands, makes *consistency* a top priority. Indeed, consistency is one of the common traits of great brands, be they corporate, product, or, in your case, personal. Yet as powerful as this institutional component is, consistency alone does not drive the success that Coca-Cola has enjoyed for over 120 years as a highly respected, well-identified, trusted brand.

Today, Coca-Cola is the most recognized and admired brand in

the world, with a market value of over $100 billion. The company has built its reputation on the shoulders of great branding discipline, standards, and execution. Over the years, it utilized a well-organized approach to brand building that is respected throughout the ranks of marketing professionals. The process begins with the consumer and follows a methodical approach to ensure a unique connection with the end user of the product. Just as Coca-Cola and other renowned brands have adopted and incorporated well-defined, disciplined policies, procedures, standards, and practices, you, too, can follow a similar approach to build a new Brand YOU. Not committing to this kind of branding discipline, standards, and great execution, on the other hand, will thwart any efforts you put forth to build your very own personal brand.

The premise of this book is that the discipline of both corporate and product brand building can be applied by anyone serious about achieving a personal transformation and who is committed to refining a unique personal brand. In presenting you with this information, we confirm a "theory of parallels": if the discipline, postulates, and best practices of branding can work for products and companies, then they can also work for individuals. Whether you are an executive, a full-time home maker, an educator, or are in any other field or in any stage of your life, the concept of creating, developing, extending, reenergizing, reinventing, and even repositioning yourself can be a powerful idea for your own growth, metamorphosis, and happiness.

Learning about great corporate, product, and even personal brand success, and applying that learning, will help you achieve your goals. In truth, we can all learn from someone else's successes and failures. Referred to as *benchmarking*, this idea works for anyone looking for a gateway to personal development. However, before diving in, you need to take some time to clarify the definition

of a *brand* and observe how a brand transcends mere product, service, or logo.

---

*The concept of creating, developing, reenergizing,
reinventing, and repositioning a Brand YOU
is a powerful idea for your own growth,
metamorphosis, and happiness.*

WHAT EXACTLY IS A BRAND?

We live in a branded world: brands to the left, brands to the right. Brands are everywhere. Consider that children who cut their finger never run to Mom screaming, "Mom, Mom, any plastic strips in the medicine case?" They ask for a Band-Aid. By the same token, how many times a day does an executive ask, "Would you please make me a Xerox copy of this?" That's even though the office copier might be a Toshiba. We sneeze into a Kleenex, clean our ears with Q-Tips, sweeten our coffee with Sweet n' Low, enjoy a bowl of Jell-O, and order a Rum and Coke at a cocktail lounge. Exhausted executives come home and say, "I'm exhausted. I'm going to soak in the Jacuzzi," even though the hot tub is made by Kohler.

Yes, we're in a branded world and brands are part of our vocabulary. We wake up in the morning on our branded mattress, brush our teeth with our preferred brand of toothpaste, soap ourselves in the shower with our favorite brand of soap, put on clothes that are labeled with the maker's name, drive to work in our branded

car, pass billboards with brand names on them, and so on. What's more, you are a brand as well. Get it?

Toyota is a highly respected automobile manufacturer. Its Camry model, considered a "subbrand," is actually a *product* of Brand Toyota. Products and brands are different. Whereas a brand is recognized and referred to by its name, a product may well be defined by its category. For instance, we refer to a brand when we ask a retail clerk if the store carries Apple computers; on the other hand, we seek a product when we look on the store shelves for a laptop computer or a specific model of Apple computer. Brands are specifically referenced by name, whereas products are often discussed by description, size, package, ingredients, and so on.

Products typically have a limited life span (i.e., the slide rule, cassette tape recorders, cell phones) while brands remain strong throughout differentiation and relevance. In fact, brands survive by keeping fresh and vibrant while not betraying core values. For any consumer product, the logo, tag line, advertising, packaging, ingredients, display, pricing, and other elements communicate the positioning. Whereas products are purchased and used, brands are sought after and chosen. In fact, advertising guru Leo Burnett once said, "Products are consumed. Brands are purchased."

Here are some more examples for further clarification:

People Consume	*People Seek, Choose, and Purchase*
Fried chicken	KFC
Beer	Budweiser
Breath mints	Tic-Tacs
Chocolates	Godiva chocolates
Safe tires	Michelin tires

There are material differences between brands of a product. Also, while a brand is a product, a product may not necessarily be a brand. So, it is fitting to start with a clear understanding of what a brand is—and isn't. When we drive by the Golden Arches, we immediately recognize this symbol as Brand McDonald's. Well, not exactly. The Golden Arches symbolize the McDonald's brand, but brand itself is far more than a graphic banner, a logo, or a design. There is no doubt that symbols are vital to extending and reinforcing a brand, but brands are more than symbols. So, what is a brand?

There are many different descriptions and definitions of a brand; in fact, there are literally hundreds, if not thousands, of books that have been written on marketing and branding, and each defines brand differently. For our purposes, the concept and definition of a brand is really quite simple. Think of a brand as a promise to a group of specific consumers, or a well-defined audience, combined with the actual experience these individuals have with the brand. This view recognizes that there is a relationship between the brand and the individual. Here, it is expressed as an equation:

Promise + experience = relationship.

A brand is identified by a distinguishing name (i.e., McDonald's) or by a symbol (i.e., the Golden Arches mentioned before) that consumers associate with a specific product, service, or—in the case of this book—person. The brand is the name we use for this product, service, or person. As well as being a promise, a successful brand has a unique personality and, ideally, a compet-

itively advantaged position in the marketplace. Delivering on this promise, via a unique personality, well-developed positioning, and relevant consumer experience, is the way the brand is established; consistent delivery of this promise, positioning, personality, and experience reinforces the brand while building brand strength and reach.

BRAND DESCRIPTIONS AND CUSTOMER PERCEPTIONS

The Internet is changing the way we live our lives. There are countless new companies that have entered the world of Internet support and service. Consequently, we use expressions such as "brick and mortar vs. click and mortar" and "e-zine" and "webinar" and "e-commerce" as important new words and phrases in our vocabulary. Perhaps no other organizations have taken this new world by storm like Google and eBay. Both of these incredibly successful enterprises have established a solid position in the marketplace by understanding their consumers and bringing innovative alternatives to traditionally mundane activities.

Searching for information, or buying and selling things, used to have space and time limitations; however, Google and eBay have created a global world that has expanded opportunities for these activities, with greater potential for future development. Researching information using the Internet has made knowledge more accessible, and on-line shopping via Internet auctions has created a larger marketplace.

Both of these companies recognize the consumer as the driving

engine behind their brands. They have transcended the world of service and product to become leading Internet industry brands, with their "product" as broad as your imagination and their "service" as wide as the world. The market capitalization of both companies is greater than many traditional brick and mortar businesses.

In our daily lives we come in contact with many products, services, and brands. Some of these items have achieved the status of recognized and/or beloved brand, occupying a favored place in our minds, hearts, and lives. Professional branders refer to this as *share of mind*. In fact, typically the greater the share of mind, the greater potential there is for gaining significant market share.

Procter & Gamble built its large laundry detergent business with brands, like Tide. In 1943, Tide was introduced as a scientific breakthrough to clean clothes better than the soap flakes of the 1920s and 1930s, combining synthetic surfactant molecules with another element to attack heavy stains. It met with huge consumer acceptance, and within weeks, Tide became the top-selling detergent; its sales and market size continue to grow today, over 60 years later. But imagine if Procter & Gamble had chosen to position Tide as the "synthetic surfactant cleaner" rather than as the "heavy-duty detergent."

Words are powerful, and they can affect the perception of a brand. Is it "new" or "improved"? Is it "new and improved"? Is it the "original," the "first," the "authentic," or "the real thing"? Is it "fairly priced," "competitively priced," "economically priced," or "value priced"? Confused? You should be. Words need to be carefully chosen to convey clear images. Yes, words are critical in the proper positioning of brands. Just compare the difference in the potential interpretation of the following words, and then imagine your

friends referring to you with these same descriptors. While they may only be words, each one helps paint a portrait of your current brand image.

How Are You Viewed by Your Friends or Family?

Assertive	Aggressive
Friendly	A pushover
Jovial	A clown
Intelligent	A nerd
Athletic	A jock
Competitive	Manipulative
Engaging	Domineering

More important, how do you *want* to be viewed by others? While you may say that you do not care what others think of you, in the context of building your brand, it really does matter. And in reality, not caring what others think of you sounds like noble positioning, but there will always be a time in your life where what others think about you is important (i.e., when your teacher is considering whether to move you as an "on the brink" student from a D to a C; or your employer is wondering whether to promote you; or your coach is thinking about bringing you up from Junior Varsity to Varsity). Perhaps, there are certain people or groups of people that you are willing to overlook because you do not value their judgment or opinion. That's fine, as long as you do not plan to target these people as part of your Brand YOU plan.

For example, you may not share the same values or perspective with some of your neighbors. In this instance, you must be

true to yourself, even if those people portray you in a light that is inconsistent with your vision for your personal brand. The key point here is that *you* have the opportunity to determine how you would like to be seen by others. You're in the driver's seat. You have control. You are also able to choose those people who are most important to you, and thereby define your target audience. Ultimately, developing a Brand YOU is about making choices regarding how you want to live your life and how to build the positive and favorable impressions you desire with your target audience.

Procter & Gamble has introduced many different improvements on Tide over the decades, based on the changing needs of consumers. Cold-water application allowed clothes to be cleaned using less energy, with great cleaning and color-retention qualities. The company has established a bond with consumers that has yielded brand loyalty and lasting success. In short, they made a promise to consumers that has been delivered through daily experience. This customer loyalty, frequently referred to as *brand insistence*, is testimony to Tide's reputation, well beyond the functional attributes of the product. Even as Tide has been reformulated to a "new and improved" position, it has stayed true to its earliest consumer commitment.

So, what is *your* brand promise and how well do you deliver on this promise? What is your brand reputation? If you ask ten close friends and relatives to list twenty-five words that they believe best describes who you are, and what your personal brand represents, it would likely be an eye-opener. Start by asking yourself what the twenty-five words are you'd use to describe Brand YOU. Be honest; don't be kind to yourself. Be frank and candid. Give yourself a valid report card on your personal brand.

ICONIC BRANDS AND WHAT THEY STAND FOR

Look at the many successful people who have reached the level of being an iconic brand. These individuals stand for specific, focused attributes. Obviously, each person is accomplished in his or her field, or at least seems to be to most people. Their uniqueness, coupled with their functional skills, represents a platform upon which even greater contributions can be built.

Beyond their jobs and areas of strength and competency, each of these iconic persons has found a purpose beyond his or her profession. Each has touched the lives of millions of people. How did they get this way? These icons understand the power of setting personal priorities, staying true to their goal of being the best in their field, and then using their power to attack their areas of passionate interest. Let's look at Brand Oprah, Brand Bono, and Brand Tiger as snapshot examples.

Brand Oprah	*Brand Bono*	*Brand Tiger*
"More Than a Television Journalist"	"More Than a Musician"	"More Than a Golfer"
Voice of Women	Social "Resolutionary"	Winner
Humanitarian	AIDS Prevention Work	Perfectionist
Activist for Change	Elimination of World	Trendsetter
Vehicle for Dialogue	Debt in Africa	Designer
	Humanitarian	Foundation for Children

These three iconic people have developed well beyond their "functional skills" of TV journalist, musician, and athlete. You, too, can extend your personal brand in a similar fashion.

Brands can be simple. Brands can be complex. Whereas most corporate and product brands are relatively simple, personal brands are usually more complex. After all, we are different brands to different audiences. For instance, a business executive might also be a husband, a father, a golfing buddy, a best friend, a community activist, and a freelance writer. Even iconic brands such as Oprah, Bono, and Tiger Woods are complex, as shown above.

Here's another example. McDonald's has established a globally iconic brand in the restaurant industry. Each day, the McDonald's system worldwide serves over 50 million people. While this is an astounding number, McDonald's views its consumer success as a brand built one customer occasion at a time. As an example, let's consider a specific "brand moment" in any McDonald's restaurant. Say, a mother with two young children enters a McDonald's with the expectation—also called a *brand promise*—of a clean restaurant serving fresh, hot food in a fast and friendly environment, at a reasonable price. She approaches the front counter, is greeted by a crew member, and gives her order, then her order is filled quickly and accurately and she is assisted to her seat by an employee. She and her children enjoy a relaxing lunch; they even spend a few minutes playing together in the Play Place area.

This mother has just had a positive experience with the McDonald's brand, and that experience is consistent with the McDonald's promise. Her relationship with the McDonald's brand is strengthened by this meal. She has chosen the McDonald's brand, and her choice has been favorably reinforced, resulting in increased brand loyalty and with McDonald's continuing to build a solid, ever-growing "share of mind" with this consumer. She is very

likely to recommend McDonald's to her friends, and she will continue to be a regular user of the brand. Her expectations were surely met—and perhaps exceeded.

If, on the other hand, her experience had been negative, the brand promise would have been broken and her relationship with McDonald's would have resulted in declining brand loyalty. Research suggests that unhappy consumers will tell many friends about their unsatisfactory experiences, while very few will share positive experiences with friends. So, a negative brand experience is costly to consumer acceptance and loyalty. Sure, poor experiences can be rectified and reversed; however, our fast-paced world typically does not provide the time necessary to give a product (or sometimes a person) that second try. Brand experiences, positive or negative, can have a lasting effect.

So what does this mean to you? Your brand—your Brand YOU—must also meet, and ideally exceed, others' expectations. Are you hoping one of your brand promises is reliability? Then why are you always late? Are you working to make sure those around you believe you are a team player? Then why do you never volunteer for a committee or activity? Is your perception of your personal brand that of a person who is logical, thoughtful, and contemplative? Then why do you make seat-of-the-pants, spur-of-the-moment decisions? Corporate, product, and personal brands all stand for something. What do you stand for? This is the threshold question that is vital for you to answer. After you complete the process that lies ahead, you will know your Brand YOU.

YOUR PROMISE TO YOUR
TARGET AUDIENCE

As an individual, you have the opportunity to identify your promise and ensure that you deliver the experience to your desired audience. What if you desire to be viewed by your colleagues as a young, upwardly mobile professional in your growing organization? Yet, you are rarely on time for meetings, and when called upon, you are unprepared to contribute any information or ideas. Unfortunately, you are providing an experience that is inconsistent with your vision of your brand promise.

The consequences of such action is that you think you are viewed as a reliable individual, yet your colleagues won't agree. In other words, your brand identity for Brand YOU is dramatically different from the brand image others have of you. However, if you are ten minutes early to each meeting, and you've brought your completed work with you, and you are ready to contribute, then you are delivering the experience that reinforces your brand promise. You have established a relationship with your team that supports your individual goals while growing your own brand.

As you establish your unique Brand YOU positioning, it will be important, nonetheless, to remain true to yourself. While you will certainly be judged by others, you must first judge yourself. Are you comfortable with the promise you have established for yourself? Can you live it? Is this promise bold, something you can be proud of achieving? Is it achievable in the time frame you've defined? Can you pass the "mirror test," each and every morning looking yourself square in the face and being totally honest with the Brand YOU you're aspiring to be? Are you realistic about your ability to fulfill your promise?

Once you are comfortable with yourself, then you can identify your target audiences and your desired effects. Given that you lead so many different lives, it will be necessary to identify those important groups you wish to influence: family, friends, co-workers, church members, and so on. These people become your target audiences. Yet, each brand promise you make should be consistent with the others you make, or you will not be building a cohesive Brand YOU. Then, of course, the proof points will be reflected in the actual experiences that you deliver to your audiences. Over time, you will see how your relationships improve and grow with those who really matter in your life.

As an individual, you have the opportunity to identify your promise and ensure that you deliver the experience to your desired audience.

Suppose you are beginning a new exercise routine that includes some jogging; when considering which running shoes to buy, what products come to mind? Obviously, you want a pair of shoes that are comfortable, give support to your weak arches, and fit the image you are looking to create. It is no surprise that Nike is at or near the top of the list of major manufacturers of running shoes. It has taken Nike years to establish itself as a performance brand for all track athletes, serious or not-so-serious. By making a commitment to innovative styles, Nike has built a relationship with millions of consumers. Obviously, Nike has conveyed to you (and millions of other consumers) exactly what they stand for. So, again, what exactly is a brand?

A brand is a promise to a group of people who have been identified as target consumers. This promise is the baseline for any brand. But in addition to this promise, a brand must deliver a personal connection or experience that reinforces the promise. Based on the experience, either a positive or a negative relationship is created with the consumer. Brand imagery is one thing in a television commercial and a very different thing as consumers experience the promise. That is why it is so important to deliver on that promise.

POSITIONING IN THE MARKETPLACE

A *logo* (short for *logotype*) is the graphic symbol of a brand, a product, or a service and it represents the specific offering of the brand. It also distinguishes competing products and companies, as with FOX Sports and ESPN, Liz Claiborne and Ralph Lauren, *USA Today* and the *Wall Street Journal*, Whole Foods and Trader Joe's, Google and Yahoo, Microsoft and Apple, Hellmann's and Kraft, Nordstrom and Saks Fifth Avenue, Bud Light and Miller Lite, McDonald's and Burger King, FedEx and UPS, Coach and Louis Vuitton, Costco and Sam's Club, Ben & Jerry's and Haagen Dazs, Dunkin' Donuts and Krispy Kreme, Target and Wal-Mart, Lowe's and Home Depot, General Motors and Toyota, Southwest Airlines and Jet Blue, Coke and Pepsi, Barnes & Noble and Borders—the list of differentiated corporate images and product brands goes on and on. Each of these brands is a high-quality, well-respected, power product and service. They all stand for something different from their competitors and are positioned differently in the marketplace.

Successful organizations choose to proactively position their brands in the marketplace rather than hope and pray that the con-

suming public will understand their core propositions. Brands can't be left to chance; careful planning and positioning are vital to a brand's success. Indeed, when a brand is represented in a manner that is either inconsistent or confusing, the buying public will draw its own assumptions that may or may not be accurate.

For example, you wouldn't want to wake up Tuesday morning and find that your favorite Starbucks has suddenly added a convenience-store hot dog grill next to the muffins and scones, promoting three hot dogs for $1.39. That would be a shock. That would be a surprise. That would be bizarre, especially to Starbucks loyalists. And that would be unacceptable. Consumers crave consistency and continuity. They do not want their beloved, trusted brands to behave differently. After all, brands (and people) are trusted because of their consistency and predictability.

Brands can't be left to chance; careful planning and positioning are vital to a brand's success.

Positioning a brand involves a combination of art and science, and it should result in a unique and meaningful distinction and personality. A successful brand stands apart from the competition and is relevant to its consumers. Great brands have a sustainable and discernible uniqueness. Whether they have what is called the "wow factor" or a point of difference, brands stand out because of their uniqueness. In fact, professional branders characterize successful brands as having both sustainable and discernible points of differentiation. Thus, positioning requires consistent communication and adaptation to a changing marketplace. Typically,

brands are viewed as high quality, great performance, very reliable, budget conscious, middle-of-the-road, and so on. Interestingly, consumers can position a brand on their own if the brand positioning isn't clear to the consumer. In the end, a brand's definition is seen through the eyes of the consumer.

The fact is that a company will position a brand in the manner it desires or else others will do that job for it. Since positioning happens in any event, why not position your Brand YOU in a space that is differentiated and desirable? Just as marketing professionals leave nothing to chance, you, too, must leave nothing to chance when developing your personal brand. Brand success doesn't happen by accident. It's accomplished by plan, by positioning.

Think, for a moment, about how various products have been positioned all around you. Nordstrom is positioned as a high-end department store while Target is a high-end mass merchandiser. Consumers shop both stores because of their respective positioning. This isn't about good or bad; it's about defining a company or product in the marketplace among competitors and positioning it in the consumer's mind. Mercedes, Cadillac, and Saab are all terrific vehicle brands, but they are positioned differently. In the category of luxury hotels, think of the Ritz-Carlton versus the Fairmont. Their positioning has been crafted by savvy branders and then judged by the consumer. For instance, choosing between the Ritz or Fairmont could get down to personal preference, because they both are positioned as luxury hotels.

For you to apply brand positioning for personal benefit, you must understand two basic cautions. First, unlike a product or corporate brand, people have baggage; they are wrapped up in emotions. Your personal history, including past successes and failures, represents an image you might want to reinforce or change in the minds of those around you. In a company, when sales decline or market penetration

drops, brand managers immediately assess the situation. They review trends, size up the competition, conduct brand equity analysis, and speak with customers and distributors in order to understand why performance has declined. To assess your brand, you'll also have to take an objective, extensive view of your strengths and weaknesses—to uncover your own deficiencies or blind spots. Don't let your emotions get in the way.

Second, successful brands cannot be, and do not try to be, all things to all people. In fact, a characteristic of well-positioned brands is their narrowed focus and specific expertise. What a great lesson for us all: to be able to focus on our goals and stand for something, not everything!

For example, Four Seasons Hotels and Resorts is a world-renowned brand of hotels that consistently delivers a premium experience. Four Seasons is willing to sacrifice the average and discount-price customer to focus on a consumer base looking for the highest level of hospitality. Similarly, Wal-Mart has a reputation for marketing and retailing national brands at low prices. It is willing to sacrifice the premium consumer looking for a one-of-a-kind diamond ring, even though its stores carry diamonds, for those customers seeking great value.

Burger King positions its restaurants to reach a target consumer it calls its "super fans"—an 18- to 34-year-old man who typically likes big portions, icy cold Coke (not Diet Coke), is usually an NFL fan, and is either a NASCAR or National Hockey League follower, or both. It's not that Burger King won't take money from a mother or a child, of course, but the marketing is directed toward the super fan. With your personal brand, you also have to focus and sacrifice. Often, people try to please everyone and in doing so overlook the most important person in the equation—themselves. Remember: it is you who you have to strive to satisfy first.

MONITORING YOUR PROGRESS

If advertising, public relations, merchandising, promotion, and branding just "talks the talk" and doesn't "walk the walk," any success will be short-lived. To determine if branding work has been successful, there must be monitoring devices among the consuming public. By analyzing reliable data, companies can choose to reposition their brands to capture growth in unmet consumer needs or reinforce existing programs.

Adjusting to consumers' needs and changes in the environment ensures that brands remain vibrant. Similarly, Brand YOU will need certain modifications as you begin to execute the plan. You may find your chosen activities not as enjoyable or successful as you thought they would be. Rather than give up on your convictions, make a small course correction.

GETTING STARTED

Just as branding professionals meticulously analyze every aspect of consumer behavior and product preferences (stereotypes, color combinations, product promises, product personality, packaging, and so on), you, too, must carefully consider all aspects of Brand YOU. Leave no stone unturned in your due diligence. Once you think you know who you are—what you represent and how you fit in the spaces you currently occupy—then think again. What new spaces would you like to occupy? How else do you want to be perceived? For what do you want Brand YOU to be known? Look at the world through other people's eyes. Get a firm grip on how they see

you. Allow this opportunity to move you one step closer to brand realization and brand optimization.

Imagine yourself as Chief Branding Officer for Brand YOU, Inc. What personal attributes are worthy of promoting? What are your challenges and what areas could you improve? What are your brand assets? What are your brand deficits? Professional branders manage a brand so that others (i.e., consumers, customers, competitors) will view that brand in a manner consistent with brand intent. *Brand intent*, simply put, is what a branding strategist wants others to believe about a brand. So, what is your Brand YOU intent? How do you want to be perceived?

Professional branders manage a brand so that others will view that brand in a manner consistent with brand intent.

This process isn't easy. For instance, it is often difficult to think of yourself in the third person. That's where imagination comes in: the more you practice imagining yourself as an objective brand manager and look at yourself as a brand instead of as "emotional you," the closer you'll get to an honest assessment. Thinking about yourself in the third person ("he," "she," "him," and "her") instead of the first person ("I" and "me") is strange, but it's the easiest way to objectively see yourself.

Once you develop a brand assessment, then you can match that assessment against your brand identity and discover any inconsistencies or gaps to be filled. The 7-Step process presented in

this book will help you get there, effectively, efficiently, and enjoyably. However, as an introduction to this process, let's look at the following example, using a fictitious person called Roger. Roger is about to begin his 7 Steps to Creating Your Most Successful Self. Here is how he views his personal brand compared with how others view his brand.

ROGER'S PERSONAL BRAND DEFINITION (ROGER'S VERSION OF HIS LIFE)

My name is Roger. I'm a married father of two young boys, am active in my church, volunteer at the local shelter, and am employed by the local office of a national real estate company as its human resources director. I spend a lot of time counseling employees and building employee esprit de corp. I am very proud of my family and thankful of how blessed I am to have a wonderful wife and partner, as well as two great sons. I pride myself on being a good listener, believe that although I don't say much and appear to be quiet, when I do talk, it's received as important. I am a highly committed team player. I enjoy going to movies, reading science fiction, playing golf once or twice a week, and gardening. I really enjoy the career I've chosen and am happy in my position and contented with my life.

Roger's Brand Assessment (Through His Family's Eyes)

Roger is very driven by his job and his pastimes. He is a good father and husband, yet we wish he spent more time at home. He is really

into his work and has a good reputation at the real estate company, but he rarely talks about his job. He is an avid golfer and is prone to spend Saturday morning with the guys at the golf course, but we don't really mind this if it makes him happy. The two boys are growing up so fast, and he frequently misses things that are going on around the house, but we manage OK. With all of his work responsibilities, his golf and community involvement, sometimes we feel our family gets the lowest priority. Yet, Roger is a good father and husband.

Roger's Brand Assessment (Through His Friends' Eyes)

Roger is a pretty nice guy who seems to spend more time volunteering at his church and at the local shelter than he does with his young children and wife. He is quiet, doesn't typically have a lot to say in conversations, seems insecure, loves bizarre science fiction novels, and spends more time on the golf course and in his garden than he does watching his kids play Little League baseball. His wife is the glue of their family. She, typically, is the primary caregiver to their children and runs the household while Roger is out in the garden, volunteering, or putting on the golf course. He works in personnel at the local real estate office and is in charge of hiring and firing. I don't think he really enjoys his job.

Roger's Brand Assessment (Through His Coworkers' Eyes)

Roger is a quiet guy who runs our company's human resources department. Although I know he is married and has children, because I've seen their photos in his office, he never talks about his family.

Any outside conversation is typically centered on his golf game or his rose garden. He is a 9-to-5 kind of person and seems to view his position more as a job than as a career. He puts up posters and notices that are supposed to motivate us, but he doesn't seem very motivated himself. I'm not sure how loyal he is to the company, and he seems to keep to himself a lot more than actively participate in company meetings and activities. He has an even disposition and never seems to get too excited about anything that happens, good or bad.

If Roger did an honest brand assessment and saw how differently others viewed his brand (brand image), he would likely be surprised—maybe even disappointed. If he wants his brand intent to be in sync with his brand image, he will have to make some adjustments to change the perceptions of those around him. For example, here might be his prescription for rebuilding his personal brand:

> I am concerned that the way my friends and coworkers saw me was inconsistent with how I thought I was perceived. My direct action includes making sure that I spend more quality time with my wife and children, even at the expense of cutting back the time I formerly spent volunteering at the church and our local homeless shelter. I will also start playing golf once a week, as opposed to twice a week, and rarely will I play on Saturday when the boys have their Little League baseball games. I will revisit my position and activities at the real estate firm and commit to doing more proactively with the employees, ensuring that they feel good about their careers and are getting the kind of education

and training programs necessary for their growth. I will also come into work a little earlier and stay a little later and will volunteer to be on a few company task forces and committees to demonstrate my support of our team. In my mind, I have always supported our company and, quite frankly, I was surprised to learn my co-workers thought otherwise. I will also try to be a lot more open and friendly to my co-workers. After all, I am in human resources. I also will start making my garden a family garden, and although they will squawk about it at first, I hope the boys will start to enjoy working together in the back yard. I will also post a bulletin board at the office to encourage associates to put family photos on display, emphasizing the importance of family at our firm—and my family photo will be the first to be put on the board. These changes aren't difficult and I'm sure they will contribute to others' looking at me differently—and in a way I'd like to be looked at.

We can all identify with Roger. Often, how we think we are perceived is dramatically better than we truly are. The third-person perspective allows you to gain insights that can convert into great ideas for improvement, and then move those great ideas into sound implementation. Consider how deep-rooted are your viewpoints, beliefs, mannerisms, feelings, and actions; they typically have been with you for as many years as you are old. When you are convinced it is time to recreate, reinvent, reposition, and reinvigorate your personal brand, make the commitment to change, to meet the challenge. It won't be easy, especially since old habits don't change easily. The health and fitness world knows the adage, "No pain, no gain"; it comes from the wisdom of Benjamin Franklin,

in his book, *Poor Richard's Almanack*. It works for body building, and it is just as true for reinvigorating your personal brand.

---

*Moving great ideas into sound implementation
is the key and the challenge.*

Some people view reinvention as a natural and necessary process; others sense there are risks attached to the activity, and still others question its sincerity. Surely it is an uncertain scenario, moving into a space requiring change in behavior or attitude. It is foreign territory, filled with unanswered questions and indeterminate results. Some will embrace the process and take the challenge. Others may ask, "What risks am I taking by doing this?"

But the more appropriate question is, "What is my risk in *not* doing this?" As with what businesses call opportunity costs, there is a cost in not doing something that could reap rewards, even when it entails some risk. Trust yourself. After you put a toe in the water, you'll acclimate to the temperature and soon move your whole body into the pool. Embrace the adventure. It's a necessary step for your future growth, prosperity, personal development, and happiness.

Inventor Thomas Edison said that "Genius is 1 percent inspiration and 99 percent perspiration." To tailor that wisdom to our situation, consider that life is 1 percent idea and 99 percent implementation. The 7 Step process, detailed in this book, shows you how to form your idea and then gives you the steps to implement it. Congratulations! You're on your way to a new Brand YOU.

KNOW WHERE YOU ARE GOING

The following quotation from Lewis Carroll's *Alice's Adventures in Wonderland* sets our stage nicely.

> "Would you tell me, please, which way I ought to go from here?"
>
> "That depends a good deal on where you want to get to," said the Cat.
>
> "I don't much care where—" said Alice.
>
> "Then it doesn't matter which way you go," said the Cat.
>
> "—so long as I get *somewhere*," Alice added as an explanation.
>
> "Oh, you're sure to do that," said the Cat, "if you only walk long enough."

If you don't know where you're going, it doesn't matter which way you go. However, in our journey—and in this brand reinvigoration process—you'll be defining your destination. With a clear destination in mind, you will be able to draw up a roadmap that will help you reach that destination. Simplicity and a proven approach guides you to the brand you want to become—or lead you to live the life you've always imagined. The beauty of this process is that you are in control all the way. You choose to include your friends or complete the journey by yourself. You can make the trip in a short period or take an extended time, so you can think deeply about your brand. However, when you follow these customized 7 Steps, you will gain the confidence and conviction to make this personal Brand YOU a reality.

Throughout this book, you will see how following the simple 7 Steps to Creating Your Most Successful Self will empower you to position your new brand easily, efficiently, effectively, and seamlessly. You will position your personal brand with purpose, in the unique space that you desire. *Managing Brand YOU* is not some seat-of-the-pants packaging effort. This book is not about what to wear and who to know. Nor is it about launching an artificial promotional campaign about you and your dreams. The 7 Steps to Creating Your Most Successful Self is based on the successful elements of corporate and product branding. Each step rises from the previous one, culminating in a tangible implementation plan—your own personal manifesto—to be in control of your future.

While it is tempting to jump steps and read the conclusion first, we advise you to follow this sequence in order to maximize your potential. For example, visualize a person who wants to reach the top of a high mountain. If that individual did not take each step from base camp to mid-camp, to summit, he or she would likely not reach the goal or the effort would take an inordinate amount of energy and time. Preparation would deal with the physical and mental challenges of such a climb. Advance work would include study of the mountain gradient and weather conditions. Additionally, clear goals would be supported by an optimal strategy, and the actual climb or implementation of the plan would be achieved with the readiness to modify as unanticipated conditions present themselves.

In mountain climbing as in all other dedicated efforts, success and security come with a step-by-step, controlled process. The climb you are about to start is no different. These seven steps will guide you to reach your personal summit—your new Brand YOU. You can be the brand that you *truly desire* if you are committed to the discipline and are honest with yourself. So, let's get started. Enjoy the journey. All aboard the personal brand wagon!

CHAPTER I

WHO AM I AND HOW DID I GET HERE?

"It is not enough to understand what we ought to be, unless we know what we are; and we do not understand what we are, unless we know what we ought to be."

—T. S. ELIOT

WHO AM I? How did I get here? The first step of the Brand YOU journey is an honest self-assessment. Consumer brand companies call this a *brand audit,* and so, true to our premise of adapting the principles and processes of corporate and product branding, we use the same term here for your first step in the 7 Steps to Creating Your Most Successful Self. Whether their product is Harley-Davidson motorcycles or Tide laundry detergent, brand managers take a thoughtful approach, stepping back and conducting a thorough assessment of the standing of their

brand before revising or enhancing a marketing plan. This step includes what professional marketers refer to as a *SWOT analysis*—short for Strengths, Weaknesses, Opportunities, and Threats. Similarly, with the Brand YOU audit you will identify and develop your own SWOT portrait. This beneficial diagnostic tool, done in a focused, highly committed, and thoroughly honest manner, will be invaluable later in the process.

YOU ARE TODAY WHAT YOU HAVE EXPERIENCED YESTERDAY

You are a function, today, of all of the life experiences you have had to date. These include, but are not limited to, your major accomplishments and significant setbacks. Now is the time to chronicle the historical mile markers in your life and the passages you have taken that have defined your current brand position. After all, your education, experience, reference points, exhilarations, and disappointments have all contributed to who you are. As poet and essayist Wendell Berry has said, "The past is our definition. We may strive, with good reason, to escape what is bad in it, but we will escape it only by adding something better to it."

You are a function, today, of all of the life experiences you have had to date. These include, but are not limited to, your major accomplishments and significant setbacks.

The Brand YOU audit is an important step. You may well carry the key to future success hidden in your past experiences, be they positive or negative. For example, let's say that as a young child you spent a lot of time outdoors. You and your family hiked and visited parks and preserves, and you enjoyed those times very much. You garnered great comfort from playing in all that nature had to offer. As an adult, you have significant stress in your life and you are anxious about each new day, about your future. Those wonderful childhood days in the woods, with hour upon hour outdoors, seem like another life. Yet reverting to this better place and unlocking the simple joys of childhood may reset the pace for your future life.

Suppose you began spending a few hours a week hiking again, going back to your beloved nature to escape the stresses of everyday life. Hey, it worked when you were younger; your youth was marked by relaxation and wonder. As a child you used to look to each new day with excitement, energy, and enthusiasm. This could be the wake-up call you've been looking for. This is exactly the rationale for the audit. Indeed, the audit may well be the first step toward your rebirth—as well as the first step in rebranding, reinventing, and reinvigorating.

A Rebranding Business Success Story

As you look at the first step of the 7 Steps to Creating Your Most Successful Self, it is important that you take a methodical approach to this self-learning. You need to work diligently to get to that "ah-Ha!" moment—maybe even experience a learning epiphany. Remember, this is not as easy as it sounds. Digging into your memory—even deeper into your psyche—and pulling up memories, feelings, and experiences (both positive and negative) is

uncomfortable. However, it is necessary if you truly want to extend, enhance, and grow your personal brand.

The Harley-Davidson Motor Company produces great products and has established and maintained a stellar reputation. However, years ago the company faced increased competition when Japanese companies like Honda, Yamaha, and Suzuki entered the American market. These three power brands began to challenge Harley-Davidson's market share, which had been built up over the years, as well as helped to hurt Harley brand loyalty. In 1969, Harley-Davidson motorcycles had become expensive, and they were perceived by consumers (i.e., brand image) as having eroded in quality. Even Harley loyalists started investigating whether the imported brands were worthy of consideration. This led to a sales decline and put Harley-Davidson in the unenviable position of facing bankruptcy.

By 1981, the company was sold to a group of investors who returned the original Harley look and feel to the product. Also, an important strength surfaced during a thorough brand analysis and audit; specifically, Harley-Davidson had a group of very loyal Harley owners. Acting on information received from their comprehensive audit, Harley-Davidson managers set up what is called the Harley Owners Group (more affectionately, HOG) in 1983. Today there are more than a million members worldwide in this group of brand-loyal owners. These Harley "super fans" feel pride in the product and consider Harley an important part of their very life and—just as important—a vital piece of the fabric of American culture. In the process, the group offered insights about the product and shared honest feedback. For example, they wanted the product to remain absolutely authentic—absolutely "all-American." They wanted it to be an American icon, true to its proud heritage, which included the sound, feel, and power of the engine. As a result,

Harley reconfigured its product, marketing, and overall brand image, and turned the company around.

By returning to the core equity of the Harley-Davidson brand and bringing HOG to life, the brand started growing again. The Harley image of the 1950s, fueled by Hollywood biker films, resulted in a Hell's Angel association with the brand, and the public viewed Harley owners as rough-riding tough guys with multiple tattoos, biker-gang affiliations, and body piercing. Talk about metamorphosis! Today the HOG is peopled from all walks of life, representing a wide range of demographics, pyschographics, even sociographics. Although Harley owners might still be seen as free spirits, they are also seen as sales professionals, doctors, lawyers, educators, and business executives. In fact, 12 percent of new Harley purchasers are women, showing also that the strong heritage and equities of this brand have transferred to a new group.

The Harley turnaround demonstrates that almost any corporate or product brand image can be dramatically altered for the better. So can your personal brand. Remember, though, that the Harley transformation didn't just happen. It was the result of a great deal of analysis (the brand audit) and a step-by-step process to rebuild the brand—the process you are embarking on in reading this book. So put your hands on the handlebars, rev your engine, and let's hit the road together.

THE FIVE DISTINCT PHASES OF LIFE

Begin your Brand YOU audit by imagining your life as a series of five distinct phases. Each phase is rich with experience and learning that influence your life, shown in Figure 1.1.

Figure 1.1. The five phases of life.

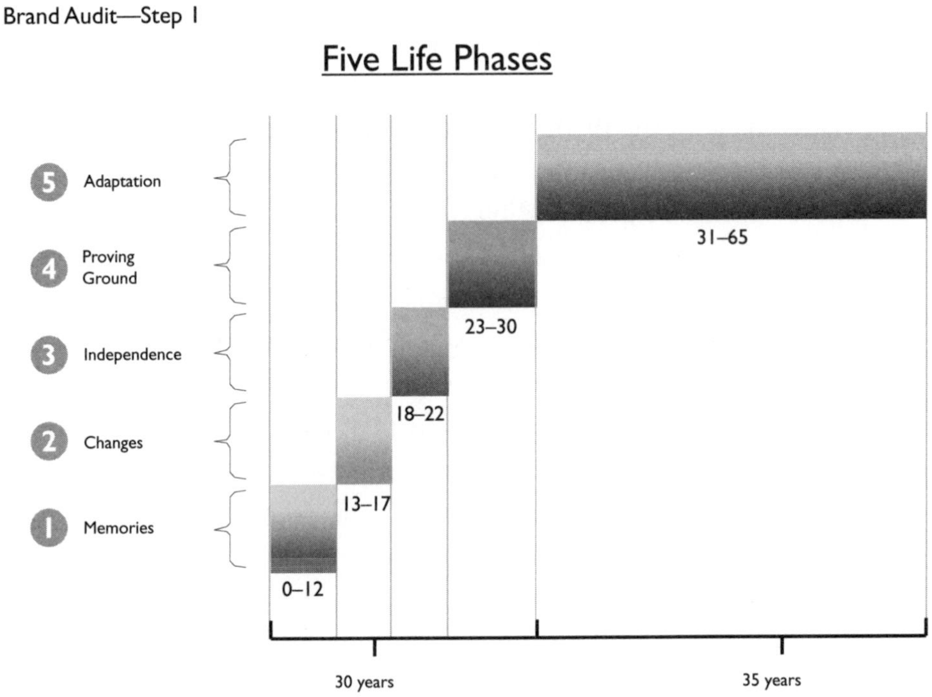

Brand Audit—Step 1

Five Life Phases

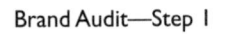

By organizing your life into these five phases, you can take stock of your life. It is interesting to note that the first three phases cover only 22 cumulative years, yet these phases have been very influential in forming Brand YOU; this will become even more apparent as you complete the audit. But now let's begin to look closely at each phase.

Phase One

Your childhood comprises the ages from birth to 12 years. You will have certain very distinct memories of this period, and they will be happy or sad and will involve friends and family because your life

at this time is closely linked to these people. Perhaps you played specific games and attended a special elementary school. Your earliest experiences and memories shape your development; you are, after all, a product of all you've experienced, touched, seen, heard, felt, and lived, especially in these early years.

Phase Two

Your teen years cover the ages from 13 through 17 and can best be characterized as years of change. These high school years are when you faced enormous challenges of acceptance and rejection, and certainly include some times of confusion and perhaps even frustration. You probably experienced mixed feelings that led, ultimately, to the level of self-esteem you feel today. Affiliation becomes an important part of your life at this point, and although you likely didn't know or use the word *inclusion*, its importance was very much a contributor to your joys and sorrows at this time. So many people's memories sting with feelings of rejection by certain groups during their teen years. After all, young people want to fit in with the crowd they view as cool or hip or savvy or smart or respected or that includes leaders—or any number of other self-defined descriptors. These high school years set a tone for the phases that follow. Though only four short years, this time has likely played a long role in shaping your current Brand YOU.

Phase Three

Your young adult years range from ages 18 through 22. This part of your life is a time when you first experienced independence. Following high school, people either move to college or take on work,

military service, or other activities. Many use this time to experiment with different lifestyles and dramatic personal growth occurs as a result. As a new, independent thinker with the responsibilities of life, you had a chance to really get to know yourself. You might have taken a trip with a group of friends to a foreign country, or you might have moved into your first apartment, or you might have started your full-time work career. During this phase you certainly reached out to new people with different ideas, and you experienced and learned so very much.

As with other phases, your accomplishments and disappointments are remembered. Even though you may have been seeking personal autonomy, a sense of connecting socially may have continued to be a theme in your life. Being rejected or accepted by those you respected set a tone for your future years. While rejection is painful at any time, during this time of independence and self-discovery, it may be even more so.

For example, if you wanted to join a specific fraternity or sorority in college, yet you did not get accepted, this rejection could symbolize personal dismissal and be interpreted as a failure. It could derail you at the very time you were entering your collegiate years and make you hesitant to join another group. Yet, if one of your friends who did not seek such membership heard of your rejection, that friend might discount this event as trivial; after all, life experiences are individual and have personal implications, just as feelings are real and can become long lasting and have unproductive results. Do you really want to carry such a grudge into adulthood? Are you really going to avoid joining organizations because of this small speed bump in your early life? The answer might very well be yes. In the end, regardless of peer-group receptivity, it is what you learn and reapply that will really matter to the

new Brand YOU. The lesson here is the key to your future: what you learn from experiences is what you do to continue moving forward, to continue growing.

Phase Four

When you become an adult, the years from age 23 to 30, you have reached the proving-ground years. You move into a period of establishing yourself as a real adult, and this likely is very important for you: to be viewed, treated, and respected as an adult. Whether this life is centered on a career, on a relationship, or on travel or otherwise, you are engulfed in proving to yourself and others that you can make it in the real world. You may hit it big early in life or you may struggle to land a respectable job. Regardless of your place in society, your independent life has entered the time when your personal brand develops significantly and you begin to make a name for yourself that will likely be attached to what your personal brand stands for.

Phase Five

The longest phase, five, encompasses age 31 through to the present. This entire phase is about adaptation. By now, you are a full-fledged, fully-functioning adult with all the responsibilities and realities that go along with adulthood. Your ability to survive and thrive is now a picture of how well you adapt to whatever life throws at you. This stage of life can involve marriage, divorce, success, failure, loss of loved ones, and everything else under the sun. Adaptation to health problems or job-related difficulties becomes a way of life, in fact. How well do you adapt? After all, many of

these occurrences are not your doing. Still, failure to adapt can be a major limiting factor to a healthy Brand YOU.

In the life span of an average adult, this longest phase represents, by far, the highest potential for growth and fulfillment. You have many years to make things happen, and you have many years to use your life experiences to help you adapt to varying conditions and challenges. It is unfortunate that too many people view this stage of life as maturity and consider it a period with little learning and when few willful changes can occur.

Not so. Even at the end of this phase opportunities abound. The list of people who have created, developed, achieved, and succeeded in their later years is incredible. Michelangelo began work on St. Peter's Basilica at age 70. Benjamin Franklin was named Chief Executive Officer of the State of Pennsylvania when he was 79. Goethe wrote "Faust" at the age of 82. Verdi composed *Otello* when he was 72. Harlan Sanders created Kentucky Fried Chicken (KFC) when he was 65. Laura Ingalls Wilder wrote *Little House on the Prairie* when she was 70 (her first book was published when she was 65). So, in the words of legendary comedian George Burns, "Everyone has to get older but that doesn't mean you have to be old."

But, wait! You're not that old yet, are you? You are, however, at a time in your life when you have acquired the experience and skills to develop and refine a brand new you—with vigor, energy, and wisdom; you work best when confronted with a challenge. This is a change that will carry you into your later years.

Whether you are in your early thirties or in more advanced years, you will be facing situations that require adaptation. Looking at this adult Phase V through an opportunistic and positive mindset will ensure you continue to develop your Brand You.

A PERSONAL SUCCESS STORY

Maya Angelou is an example of someone who overcame many real challenges in her life to become one of the most respected American poets and humanitarians of modern time. She was born on April 4, 1928, in St. Louis, Missouri, as Marguerite Ann Johnson. When she was 3 years old, her parents divorced, and she and her 4-year-old brother, Bailey, were sent to live with their grandmother in Stamps, Arkansas. She took up dance classes while living with her grandmother. The children were sent back to live with their mother, who was now in California; while there, Maya was sexually abused at the age of 7 by her mother's boyfriend. After sharing this incident with her brother, who conversely told her uncle, Maya's uncle killed the child molester. For the next five years, Maya did not speak, since she believed that her words led to the death of another person and she felt great guilt. Maya returned to live with her grandmother in Stamps, where she began speaking again and was introduced to classical literature.

Later Maya moved in with her father, where she was assaulted by his girlfriend. She then ran away from home and lived in a junkyard with many other homeless children. During the month she lived there, Maya met children from other ethnicities and backgrounds, all sharing the same goal—survival. She would later share in her autobiographical work *I Know Why the Caged Bird Sings* that this period had a significant influence on her life and her mindset. Living in what she called a "community of equals," she grasped a deeper understanding of people and their unconditional acceptance of her for just who she was.

Maya experienced life without condemnation, and this environment taught her the lessons of acceptance, open-mindedness, and

tolerance. After dropping out of high school, she worked as the first African-American female streetcar conductor in San Francisco. She eventually returned to high school and graduated three weeks before her son Guy was born. Maya supported Guy and herself in various jobs, including that of cocktail waitress, dancer, and cook. By the time Maya was 16 years old, she had already been through more pain and suffering, and had met more challenges, than most people endure in a lifetime.

Consider, now, what Maya Angelou's childhood memories represent. Think about how she spent her teenage years, then consider the life lessons and learning she would carry with her for the remainder of her life. Through it all, she acquired personal strength and wisdom. Obviously, she is a survivor with significant personal resilience. She has learned the power of language and the gift of tolerance.

Maya married a Greek sailor, Tosh Angelos, in 1952; they divorced three years later. At this time she formally adopted the name *Maya* (her childhood nickname) and *Angelou* as a twist on her former husband's name. She used this professional name in 1954–55 when she performed in nightclubs and toured Europe in *Porgy and Bess*. She became a student of modern dance and recorded her first album, *Calypso Lady*, in 1957. Maya relocated to New York City, where she acted in off-Broadway productions and joined the Harlem Writers Guild. She honed her writing skills among an increasing group of young black writers and artists engaged in the civil rights movement.

She met and fell in love with the South African civil rights activist Vusumzi Make, and they moved to Cairo, Egypt, in 1960 where she became editor of a weekly newspaper, *The Arab Observer*. In 1963 they moved to Ghana, where she served as an instructor and assis-

tant administrator at the University of Ghana's School of Music and Drama; she continued her literary work there as well. It was during this time in Africa when Maya became fluent in several languages. Think of the irony: for five years as a child she had been mute and now she was a linguist. Perhaps this is not ironic at all, but instead is a reflection of the broadmindedness she learned as a child.

This is a long story, but it has great relevance to your brand audit. Reflect on how Maya Angelou's brand audit might read for her years of teenage independence and young-adult proving ground. After all, when she went to Africa, she was only in her early thirties. With her son, Guy, she had to face many adult issues while others were finding their way through simpler times.

When Maya returned to America in 1964, she planned to support Malcolm X as he was building the Organization of African American Unity. His assassination ended all dreams of this organization, and this event was yet another blow to Angelou. In spite of this loss, she shifted her energy to work with Dr. Martin Luther King, Jr., serving as Northern Coordinator for the Southern Christian Leadership Conference. Dr. King's assassination, on her birthday in 1968, was another huge setback that left her demoralized, depressed, and emotionally demolished.

Somehow, through the urging of her friend, novelist James Baldwin, she began to write her story, which gave her a certain peace. Maya's writings elevated her to a person with national stature, and more publications followed, including *Gather Together in My Name, Singin' and Swingin' and Gettin' Merry Like Christmas, The Heart of a Woman, All God's Children Need Traveling Shoes, A Song Flung Up To Heaven,* and *The Collected Autobiographies of Maya Angelou*, established Angelou as a world-renowned thinker, writer, and literary force in this world.

WRITE YOUR OWN SUCCESS STORY

Who would have thought that this young girl would grow into an American icon? From pauper to Poet Laureate, Maya Angelou developed her highly respected personal brand. Your early phases of life likely were not as challenging, and your achievements may not end up being as grand, but you also have a unique collection of experiences that have taken you to the Brand YOU are today. The trick is, how do you turn your experiences and encounters into real achievements and know-how? What core theme describes each phase of your life and what lessons can you bring forward? How do you use those positive and negative experiences as a springboard for getting you where you want to be?

For instance, how do you use each year that passes? Have you learned during each phase of your life and incorporated what you have learned into your life plan? Or have you allowed setbacks to become barriers to your greatness today? Do you follow your passions and stand up for what you believe? Or do you follow the lead of others? Let Maya Angelou serve as a motivator for you to find the drive within you. If she could overcome all of her many life challenges, you have that same ability to rise to the occasion. Each of us has the power to meet the challenges we face and create our own successful future. Take the time now to complete your own brand audit, being detailed and thorough—after all, you never know which small detail from your past will become the turning point to your future.

It's a pity so many people think that the older they get, the less apt they are to change and grow; most can't even dream of reinventing their persona or retailoring their personal brand. Many people also have allowed a past bad experience, a failure, or an embarrassment to hold them back. Think about it: why should something

that happened during four years of high school define your entire life? Not making the high school football team certainly had to be a disappointment. Failing to win the election for class president probably was a real setback. Finishing low in your class academic ranking most likely brought on a period of disillusionment. However, you can use these bad experiences to help you grow.

You can choose to move beyond those frustrations. After all, what are the chances that someone in your life today is even aware of that incident in your past? Don't replay those old tapes in your mind—and don't repeat them in your behaviors. Try on a different pair of glasses.

Look at your major successes and failures and see what they taught you. How did you behave during those moments? Did you see the bright future ahead when you succeeded at something? Or did you think only of doom and gloom after a defeat? You might miss noticing a great new strength that has been dormant all these years. Open your mind and expand your positive realm. Take these personal setbacks and turn them into favorable forces in your life. You get the point: live and learn. That's the model.

Remember, you can be in control of your future, based on how you choose to handle victory and adversity as they arise. Facing reality will allow you to shift into high gear and transform Brand YOU. Use your experiences, positive or negative, to craft new ways to reposition yourself and your personal brand for future success, satisfaction, and achievement.

You can control your future based on how you handle victory and adversity.

STEP ONE: THE BRAND YOU AUDIT

Okay, now that you understand the phases of life, it is time to get to work on your Brand YOU audit. This begins with self-awareness. Take the time to go back to your earliest childhood memories. Log every significant event, every achievement, every affiliation or activity that you can recall. Recognize the times of pride and of disappointment. Prepare this log through your five life phases, up to the present day. We've included the Brand YOU audit worksheet (Figure 1.2) that is designed to guide you through this step. It will help you organize your thinking and prod you to answer some important questions about yourself. This is personal. It is private. And it can only help you if you commit to absolute, no-holds-barred honesty. Is this difficult? Yes. Will it all be worth it? Absolutely!

Realize that this audit may take you days to complete, maybe even longer. Some people choose to complete it with the help of a trusted friend or family member, while others prefer to be completely private. Whichever method you select, focus on honesty and comfort. You may find a vacation away from your usual routine is the best time to do the audit; you might be better able to relax and think freely. You might do the audit in sections, working on one period for a time and then leaving it for a while and returning to it a few hours or days later. The key is to be honest, accurate, and as complete as possible. If you are a multitasker, you might keep a note pad handy, so that while you're sitting at your desk, or on a plane, or watching television, you can jot down incidents and feelings that you can transfer to the worksheet with greater detail later on.

The Brand YOU audit begins with a comprehensive survey of your life experiences, without regard to importance or relevance. Then, you identify the core themes from each life phase. Finally, you

Figure 1.2. The Brand YOU audit worksheet.

	AGES 0–12 MEMORIES	AGES 13–17 CHANGES	AGES 18–22 INDEPENDENCE	AGES 23–30 PROVING GROUND	AGES 31–PRESENT ADAPTATION
Activities					
Affiliations					
Successes					
Failures					
Disappointments					
Satisfactions					
Anything Else of Importance					
Core Themes					
Life Learning					

develop these core themes into life learning. As you can see in Figure 1.2, the worksheet includes all three steps. Fill in the spaces directly on the page so that the book becomes your handbook for building your new Brand YOU. If you need more space, add pages. The more comprehensive your audit, the quicker you will move to the next step of the process.

Filling out the brand audit is an introspective experience, and it may reopen old wounds. Whether it's a minor childhood disappointment or a personal failure in an important endeavor, you need to face the music and dance; ultimately, you will find this cathartic and, in the long term, it will help you come to grips with the injuries that have put you in the place you are now. While no one can undo the past, everyone has the potential for a bright future once the baggage has been discarded. Facing those lingering problems will provide the long-term relief you need to achieve your new Brand YOU.

Unfinished business is a major barrier to achieving your true potential.

A SAMPLE AUDIT: BRAND JULIE

Here's a sample of how the audit is done (see Figure 1.3). In this case, we've given the portrait of Julie, a 28-year-old professional who has led a relatively successful life to this point, yet she believes there must be more to life than she is currently enjoying. She has decided to examine her life through the lens of our 7 Steps to

Figure 1.3. Brand JULIE audit worksheet.

	AGES 0–12 MEMORIES	AGES 13–17 CHANGES	AGES 18–22 INDEPENDENCE	AGES 23–30 PROVING GROUND
	Born, Atlanta, GA Brother, John Happy at the park Family cook-outs Girl Scouts Church activities	Father as high school teacher Report card tension Academic underachiever Heavy pressure from Dad The "perfect" brother Parents divorce Isolation Did not fit into high school Loved being in the school play Mother as friend High school graduation	Took job at local retailer Fell in love with Don Married Don 3 years of unhappy marriage Abusive husband Divorce Asst. Manager of department Set up personal apartment Brother as partner and perfect marriage	Moved into new apartment, alone Few girlfriends for weekend activities No serious boyfriends No serious career options beyond the retailer
Core Themes	Carefree times Happy with brother Mother as best friend	Pressure to perform Brother as competitor Misfit Nothing is forever (divorce of parents) Loved the theater Glad to be out of school	No more school First love is husband Nothing is forever (divorce) Good worker Respected at work Perfect brother syndrome	Starting over at 23 What is my future?
Life Learning	Enjoyed organized group activities (Girl Scouts, church functions)	Pressure is NOT motivating I can survive anything I enjoy being on stage as an actor I can trust Mom	I am very responsible I want someone to share this life with I will not settle for this abuse I have performed in the business world I don't like it when people compare my life with that of my brother	I can survive on my own I am strong I am ambitious I can envision a better tomorrow I am happy for my brother I am committed to a better future

Creating a More Successful Self process. Throughout this book, you will follow this fictional person through the process, allowing you to see how the 7 Steps to Creating a More Successful Self can work for you personally. Note that, because Julie is 28 years old, there's no need to include the sixth column, for ages 31 and over.

Julie's Background Story

Julie was born in Atlanta, Georgia, and has a brother, John, who is two years older than she is. As a young child, Julie enjoyed playing in the park with her family and has fond memories of her father's working in his workshop during the weekends. Her mother was a stay-at-home mom while her dad was a teacher at the local high school. Julie was very involved in Girl Scouts and active in her church as a child. She and her brother were close and they remain close friends today.

Julie was an average student academically, always struggling to make the grades her father expected of her. Consequently, she was always fearful of the dreaded report card in junior high school. While her brother, John, seemed to breeze through with top grades, she always worked hard to complete her classwork. Julie compensated for this academic shortfall by developing a very close relationship with her mother. After all, her mother was always there for her while her father was constantly awaiting the next report card.

During high school, her parents went through a difficult divorce owing to many irreconcilable issues. Her father was committed to his high school teaching career and eventually became a high school principal in a nearby town. Julie and her brother stayed with their mother, and it seemed that the family she had counted on was suddenly disbanded. As a high school student, Julie struggled to find herself socially. While she was accepted by a handful of friends,

she was not involved in any activities and felt isolated from most other kids. Ironically, one day, a teacher suggested she consider joining the drama club, which was seeking another actor for the spring play. To her amazement, she was selected and played an important secondary role in the performance. She loved it. This was just the tonic she had hoped for throughout high school. While an outcast in class, Julie was now important—now a "somebody" on stage—and she was as happy as she had ever been in her life.

Julie graduated from high school and decided to skip college in order to work for a large department store as a retail sales clerk. The money was good, and she was now free from the grading system, pressures, and cliques of high school. Her work ethic was second to none. Julie was always on time and ready to work whenever the manager scheduled her, and she quickly rose to assistant manager of the department. She met a guy in a neighboring store in the mall, and within two years they were married. She and her new husband, Don, had a lot in common. He also skipped college in order to work in a local tire store. During their modest wedding, Julie was reunited with her brother, who had just completed college and was beginning his career as an accountant at a prestigious public accounting firm. She also saw her long-estranged father and she felt melancholy about her childhood and her difficult high school years.

Less than three years after their wedding, she and Don were calling it quits. There were constant fights over money, and Don was abusive to Julie. The only saving grace was that there were no children in their marriage. After years of arguments and pain, the two divorced, and Julie found herself on her own once again. At 23, Julie was moving into a new apartment, starting over, and wondering what was ahead for her. Some of her friends had recently graduated from college, and she was beginning to question many of her earlier decisions. Meanwhile, brother John had just passed the CPA

exam and had been named partner at his accounting firm. John and his wife, Kate, had a seemingly perfect marriage.

For the next five years, Julie continued to work for the same retailer and had become manager of her department. She had dated a few guys, but none of them seemed serious about a long-lasting relationship. She continued to live in her apartment and made a few friends within the complex to enjoy weekend activities with. All in all, her life had become quite predictable and even a bit depressing at the young age of 28.

Julie knew she had to take control of her life, but she had no clue where she should start. She did not have a college education, she had worked for the same retailer since graduating from high school, and now she was divorced. What kind of future could she envision that was brighter than the course she was on already?

Her Brand JULIE audit proved to be a source of inspiration. She was able to uncover some hidden life learning that could help her to reposition Brand JULIE.

Julie's Future

Equipped with her Brand JULIE audit, she is now preparing to move into the second step of identifying her current image. Julie's story and audit is here as an example of how to complete your own audit and to give you inspiration for carrying on to the next step in the process.

IT'S FINISHED; WHAT'S NEXT?

Once you have completed this self-assessment, you will have a clear picture of who you are and how you got here. Realize that

the most important part of your life lies ahead, not behind you. Yet recognizing the building blocks of your life will help you understand your present situation and provide insight on how to plot a course for the future Brand YOU you're hoping to become.

Now that you have completed your assessment, you are ready to identify the clear and definite patterns in your life. What stands out for you? What core themes begin to surface? Were you a person who has enjoyed community service? Are you a natural-born leader? Have you uncovered trends among events that seemed random before? These patterns will become evident when you step back and review the brand audit.

In fact, the audit will bring to the surface many different matters in your life. Having identified the core themes, you will now recognize the life learning that has come from these themes. Successful people have the ability to turn negatives into positives; they see the learning that can come with each predicament and leverage this learning to move forward in their lives.

Equipped with a completed brand audit, you are now ready to move to Step 2. Each step from now on will build on the work you have done in this chapter. Take time to review your worksheet and ensure that you have been true to yourself and accurate in describing your life to date. Remember, if the foundation is shaky, the building will collapse.

Congratulations! You have taken a long look in the mirror and survived. Believe it or not, this may have been the most challenging and reflective part of the process. Now, take a deep breath, relax, and feel good about yourself, the progress you're making, and the great start you've made on the journey.

CHAPTER 2

WHAT DO I STAND FOR TODAY?

STEP TWO: ASSESS YOUR BRAND **YOU** *IMAGE*

"Could a greater miracle take place than for us to look through each other's eyes for an instant?"

—HENRY DAVID THOREAU

HOW ARE YOU PERCEIVED *today* by your friends and colleagues? Regardless of your answer, their view of you is the result of existing elements that define who you currently are as well as the messages you've sent them in the past, both verbally and nonverbally, wittingly and unwittingly. Having just completed the Brand YOU audit, you now can take stock of how you are perceived by others. In Step 2 of the 7 Steps to Creating a More Successful Self, you have a chance to measure your self-perception against the perceptions and views of friends and colleagues. Like it or not, it is the views of those around you that define your personal brand image.

They, the amorphous pronoun, think this about you. *They*, the anonymous crowd, believe you stand for—whatever. *They*, your friends and family, define you as . . . and respect you because . . . and *they* believe you're important because of. . . . *They* can't be ignored. Step 2 is the point at which you start to understand your currently perceived image. Later in the process, you will examine the Brand YOU identity you want to create. And over time, both your image and your identity will shift so your Brand YOU journey is perpetual. Your image today may be different from what it will be in two years' time, and this will have an impact on how you refresh your identity then.

BRAND IMAGE VERSUS BRAND IDENTITY

A brand image, be it a product or a person, is always defined through the eyes of others. That's the definition of *brand image*: how your brand is currently perceived by those around you. That perception may be very different from your *brand identity*, which is what you would like to stand for and what you'd prefer to project to others.

The brand image is the total picture of how consumers think of a brand. In the case of personal branding, it is how others think of you, if they think of you at all. This perception compares the promise a brand makes with the delivery of that promise. For example, if a brand promises a high-quality experience and then falls short, the image is tarnished. Conversely, if a brand overdelivers on its promise, the image is polished. In fact, brand image is something that's always on the move. Each day, brands are either being

polished or being tarnished in the eyes of consumers. So, the intent here is to constantly polish Brand YOU and ensure that your vision (and aspiration) for your new personal brand (brand identity) anticipate what *they* will think (brand image).

Brand image is the total picture of how others think of a brand. It is also how others think of you.

The very notion of seeing yourself through the eyes of others is potentially disconcerting. When personal cameras shot 35 mm film, back in the days before digital photography became the standard, you would go on vacation and later anxiously await the prints back from your local photo shop or even the one-hour retailer. When you finally had those prints in your hand, how often did you look at yourself in those photos and say, "That can't be me! There's no way I look that fat . . . or that old . . . or that tired." Seeing a photo of yourself is a lot like seeing yourself through someone else's eyes. It's not always pleasant, especially if you anticipated a flattering shot of yourself on the beach. No worries. Everyone has gone through this eye-opening experience.

That rude awakening is the kind of drill corporate, product, and personal branders usually experience. The key question is, "How am I perceived through another's eyes?" Whereas a marketing executive might schedule focus groups or mall intercepts, or conduct surveys to find out how a brand is viewed, your personal branding challenge is to conduct a mini-survey that provides the same type of information, obviously without the marketing budget or corporate structure behind you. Family and true friends will tell

you the truth if you ask them. The adage "The truth always hurts" isn't necessarily the case; however, the truth is vital to understanding how others see you. The more you can find out the truth, the better focused you'll be on your Brand YOU process. But let's look at a few examples.

The Volvo Brand Image

Volvo has developed a reputation as a reliable and safe car. Its brand image is important in the company's maintaining a strong position in the marketplace, and it also serves as a sustainable, discernible point of uniqueness. For Volvo, passenger safety is the overarching theme that has framed its image. While Volvo delivers solid vehicle performance, Volvo engineers constantly study features that help contribute to greater automotive safety. From multiple air bags, to skid-free braking, to greater handling and improved visibility, all safety factors must be routinely monitored. By owning this brand image of safety, Volvo has successfully permeated its product development and consumer messages. The company delivers on its promise, and consumers looking especially for safety in a car are attracted to the brand. Volvo's brand identity and its brand image are seamless and in sync. In fact, since 1944, Volvo has introduced over 40 lifesaving innovations to ensure the safety of its customers.

Imagine if, for some unforeseen reason, the safety of passengers in a vehicle produced by Volvo is compromised, there would be a material breakdown in the promise and Volvo's image would deteriorate quickly. While it has taken Volvo many years to create this image, it would be only a few days before consumers would lose their trust in the brand. This is why great branders such as Volvo *constantly* review the "snapshots" through their consumers' lenses;

and it's why the company also seeks feedback from outsiders, who provide their views on the brand's perception by customers.

All great branders desperately seek to understand the consumers' feelings, viewpoints, and perspectives on their brands. You're your personal brand manager, you also need to seek feedback. You need to know what *they* think of you.

The Johnson & Johnson Brand Image

The pharmaceutical giant Johnson & Johnson faced a brand image crisis in 1982, with the discovery of cyanide in capsules of its Extra Strength Tylenol. Seven people died during this tragic incident of product tampering. Given that the company is a consumer-focused firm, this incident was handled with distinction, resulting in an industry-changing approach to such challenges of tampering and terrorism. Immediately upon learning of the situation, Johnson & Johnson proactively alerted the public through mass-media efforts. This was followed by a product recall of over 31 million bottles, which cost the company more than $100 million. The company then stopped selling capsules and replaced all Extra Strength Tylenol capsules with caplets. This decision further protected consumers from product-tampering attempts.

During this crisis, Johnson & Johnson successfully used the event to demonstrate its commitment to the safety of its customers. Throughout the period, the company maintained its customer focus and built on its credibility, as well as bolstered brand confidence and loyalty. In spite of a short-term decline in stock price and decrease in market share, Johnson & Johnson enhanced and rebuilt its brand image over the long term. The company eventually introduced a tamper-resistant package that set a new standard for over-the-counter drug safety.

This example demonstrates the power of taking bold action during challenging times. By maintaining open lines of communication and standing behind its customers, Johnson & Johnson was able to survive the incident as well as improve its brand image. For the individual as well, brand perception and image can be turned around through strategic repositioning and sound execution. If brand image is the totality of others' perceptions of you, then how strong is your brand image? Everyone has ups and downs in their lives, yet many people try to cover up the "downs" rather than deal with them head on. In the Johnson & Johnson example, company leaders chose to face the issue straight ahead, take the necessary actions, spend whatever necessary to eradicate the issue, and communicated aggressively. How well have you dealt with the "downs" in your life? Do you procrastinate? Do you go into denial? Do you hide from realities? Or do you meet your challenges and shortcomings head on and work toward improvement?

The Disney Brand Image

Walter Elias Disney, born December 5, 1901, in Chicago, Illinois, lived his entire life in a manner that created a positive image for himself and for those he touched. In fact, Walt Disney became, in a true sense, America. Walt spent his childhood in Marceline, Missouri, where he developed his early hand at drawing. In fact, by the time he was 7, he was already selling sketches to friends and neighbors. Even during his school days, Walt was prone to draw pictures of animals and the outdoors. He fell in love with trains when he worked during a summer for his Uncle Mike Martin, who was an engineer, a love that he enjoyed throughout his life.

When he was a teen, Walt attempted to enroll in the military, but he was rejected as below minimum age. In spite of this, Walt joined

the Red Cross and went to France, where he drove an ambulance that was eventually covered with his cartoon drawings. Upon his return to the United States, he pursued his passion for commercial art. By the time he was 22, Walt Disney had experimented with animation, had created *The Alice Comedies* films, and had survived his company's bankruptcy. Disney's taste for risk taking was not diminished by the trial and failure of his early endeavors. His brother Roy contributed $250, and an additional $500 loan, to start up another film operation in their uncle's garage in California. Well, as you know, Walt Disney became a movie and animation industry icon, as well as a global force in the world of entertainment. His vision of a "Disney land" came out of a desire to have a place where he could play with his two daughters. In 1955, Disneyland Park opened and set a new standard for amusement parks.

While Walt Disney's commercial success is widely known, what perceptions did other people have of him? It is clear that he was an imaginative boy who remained forever curious. He was not afraid to take risks, which frequently led to short-term failures. Yet he always bounced back, flush with new ideas. His love for his wife and family permeated his work, and he always placed time with his family above the social networking of Hollywood. His family-man image played out in his films as well as at the clean and safe amusement park he created for family entertainment. As a business person, Walt was known to be demanding, and even demonstrated his temper at times. Yet these moments would quickly give way to the real work at hand, which was his commitment to art and to making magic on the screen. One need only to watch some of his animated movies to get a feel for Walt the man as well as Brand WALT DISNEY. Clearly, Walt Disney's personal brand image can be described as a person committed to quality, invention, imagination, and happiness. Today's Walt Disney Company reflects

the image of its founder. With a portfolio of four business segments, including studio entertainment, parks and resorts, consumer products, and media networks, you may wonder how a central brand essence could prevail. The Walt Disney Company recognizes that its image reflects unequaled entertainment for the entire family. Over the decades, the company could have shifted to a different type of entertainment in pursuit of a larger bottom line. But by maintaining its wholesome brand image, Disney has prospered and grown both the company and its brand. Throughout its portfolio of companies, Disney appeals to consumers of all ages with products and services for the changing family.

A dedicated father and husband, Walt Disney injected his family values into his work, which resulted in a positive image in the community and in the entertainment world. Now, imagine a new Brand YOU as so committed to your inner drive that you're willing to take the necessary risks, to bounce back from failure, and build the life of your dreams. Visualize your new Brand YOU image with a high regard from others, owing to your dedication to your personal priorities. You don't need to create an animated film to have the same kind of reputation and image. You can develop the image you desire by being true to yourself and portraying this in your beliefs, words, and deeds. Will it take work? Absolutely. Will it require commitment and consistency? Absolutely. But the commitment and hard work required to build a new Brand YOU is a labor of love and incredibly important for your life's plan.

The Gandhi Brand Image

Another person who created a recognizable brand image with others is Mohandas Karamchand Gandhi, commonly known as Mahatma Gandhi. During his life, Mahatma Gandhi made a lasting

impact on humanity. Born in 1869, in India, Gandhi was educated at University College, London, where he studied law. After being admitted to the British bar, he returned to India to establish a law practice in Bombay. Two years later, Gandhi went to South Africa, where he faced the realities of discrimination and was even imprisoned on several occasions. Gandhi developed his idea of passive resistance with his *Satyagraha*, which means "truth and firmness." In his mid-forties, he returned to India, where he became engaged in the country's struggle for home rule. Over time, Gandhi pursued his peaceful revolution of Satyagraha, which led to a movement for *Swaraj* (self-government), and this economic revolution spawned independence within the Indian population, resulting in Gandhi's embodying the country's symbol of Indian freedom.

Throughout his life, Gandhi stayed true to his spiritual life of prayer, fasting, and meditation. He refused material possessions, and he dressed in the traditional loincloth of the lowest stratum of Indian people. His calm ability to persuade others ultimately led to political and spiritual command of India. A man of the people, Gandhi certainly did not follow the Brand YOU process, yet it is easy to see how he maximized each of his five life phases. He was a constant learner, and was committed to his core values and principles. His influence in the history of modern India is indisputable; he continued to have a positive impact until his death in 1948. His life, which spanned seven decades, is a tribute to a gentle leader who lived each year with purpose and dedication to his beliefs, and to fellow countrymen and women.

Gandhi's personal brand image is a reflection of the life he led. His intelligence and resistance to civil injustice guided his life and influenced how he was perceived by others. Not only was he able to lead a nation with his political and spiritual savvy, but he did so while building his image as a leader among the people. Gandhi's selection

of traditional loincloth as his dress reinforced his brand image as a common citizen. Even his fasting as a form of social rebellion was consistent with his peaceful social statement. His image of civil disobedience galvanized the nation and led to its ultimate independence from British rule. Gandhi's principles, and the image he stood for, became a driving force in the American civil rights movement as well. It is well accepted that Gandhi's activities were an inspiration to Dr. Martin Luther King, Jr.

Obtaining Feedback on Your Image

So, how can you go about learning how others perceive you? This step can be as easy or difficult as you choose. A three-step approach will assist you in identifying your brand image.

The first step is to write down the various comments or pieces of feedback you have received from others over the past couple of years. You may be surprised just how reflective these small pieces of feedback might be. Generally, people receive feedback each day. It comes in the form of passing comments, nonverbal signs, and responses to statements you make. English clergyman and metaphysical poet George Herbert wrote, "The best mirror is an old friend." Think back over the past couple of years and remember interactions you had with friends, colleagues, and family members. This can give you a good indication of how others have viewed you. Have your friends given you any clues about how they think of you? It could be as straightforward as a comment like, "I haven't seen you much lately. What have you been doing?" Have your colleagues at work commented, "You don't seem to be very focused; is everything all right at home?" Both of these questions can help you look at yourself.

The second step is to call in a few chips from your loved ones and friends. Sometimes the most direct approach is the best approach.

Why not speak to your closest loved ones, family members, siblings, children, and best friends? Share with them that you're going through a personal development program designed to audit your life and help you better understand ways you can grow and perhaps improve your life's activities. Share with them your quest for a better Brand YOU.

Declaring your commitment to improvement is a positive thing that true loved ones and friends will support. Ask them to write a few sentences or a paragraph about you. Give them a little guidance, such as:

"John, you've been one of my closest friends for decades. I truly respect you, like you, and treasure our friendship because it has always been based on honesty and sharing. I'm going through a very positive and important personal development activity. I'm trying to analyze how I'm perceived by others so I can take stock in what I call my 'personal brand' and make decisions about ways I can improve, or change positively if needed, and grow.

"I'd be very appreciative if you could write a paragraph or two on how you see me. I won't be offended by anything you say. In fact, I'll be thankful for your candor. Here's an example: Do you see me as witty? Silly? Pragmatic? Opinionated? A team player or a loner? I'd really appreciate your help, friend."

Ask the friends to give you their candid viewpoints on the Brand YOU they know and perhaps love. Here are some more questions to suggest. You may find that your friends are most comfortable providing their feedback in writing or through a face-to-face interview.

➤ How do you perceive me? How do you think others perceive me (Be specific; are you referring to co-workers, neighbors, or whom?)

- ➤ What kind of image do others have of me?
- ➤ What kind of image do I project?
- ➤ What do you believe are my top three personal strengths?
- ➤ What three areas in my life need improvement or development?
- ➤ What have I not asked you that you think I should know about how I am viewed by others?

Yes, the best mirror is a friend, and if you can stand their being honest with you, you can come closer to understanding how you are perceived. However, it is often difficult to get insightful comments from friends when you merely ask them to share how you may be perceived by others. Obviously, their natural response is to relate how well you are liked by others or how respected you are within the community. Putting people on the spot with this type of question makes friends uncomfortable and you may not get the honest feedback that you are seeking.

In addition to the above questions, which are more general, the following will help you elicit more specific comments from trusted friends (you should also ask yourself these questions, and answer honestly).

- ➤ Am I reliable?
- ➤ Do I overpromise and underdeliver in my commitments?
- ➤ Am I punctual?
- ➤ Do I show respect to others?
- ➤ How often do I reach out to others?
- ➤ Am I trustworthy in my dealings with others?
- ➤ Am I manipulative or sincere with others?
- ➤ How do I look in the mirror?
- ➤ Do I seem happy?

➤ Am I mean to others?

➤ Am I optimistic?

➤ Am I a team player?

➤ Do I enjoy social activities?

➤ Do I ever take time to develop myself in areas of personal interest?

➤ Do I listen to what others have to say?

➤ Am I too judgmental?

➤ Am I too self-centered?

You get the picture. Create more personally relevant questions that you may want to ask yourself. When you discuss your image with a friend or family member, be open to whatever comes out of such a conversation. Do not become defensive or try to rationalize the feedback. Take written notes for you to refer to later. Listen intently and probe for greater clarity. Be appreciative of their help and of the personal risk they are taking just by being open with you. Regardless of the comments, criticism, compliments, and recommendations that come forth, consider yourself extremely fortunate. Very few people have such allies willing to contribute to a better Brand YOU.

Certainly, this process is not meant to provide psychological counseling or change your overall personality. Yet, without some understanding of where you are today, you will lack a key to building a new Brand YOU. So, the third approach for you to consider is to use some tools that will help you better understand how you are seen by others.

There are many different programs on the Internet that may aid in self-assessment. For example, the Myers-Briggs Foundation has developed a simple yes/no questionnaire that helps you identify your specific personality type, and this is available online. This

test identifies 16 different types of personalities, ranging from Introvert to Extrovert, based on how you deal with information, decisions, and structure. Recognizing these traits may help you better understand how you interact with others and how you may be perceived by others.

Take your self-assessment using the best available tools for your situation. Find Internet resources or Google "personality tests." Some of these tests require financial payment while others are free. Even the simple yes/no 72-question Myers-Briggs survey mentioned above will give you a good start at identifying your brand image. By bundling these three approaches, you will be closer to understanding how others view you and how they perceive your personal brand.

THE BRAND YOU IMAGE WORKSHEET

Figure 2.1 is the Brand YOU image worksheet.

This isn't a time to be timid or overly sensitive. Accept the fact that life is all about continuous improvement. It is a myth to assume that success is in the hands of the "learned." Success is in the hands of the "learning." Life is a continuous learning process. These image reports can go a long way toward helping you build the Brand YOU you want to develop. When all is said and done, you will face the fact that you cannot make everybody happy all the time. So, some of the comments from your friends or colleagues may not even matter to you. After all, if you believe Brand YOU can win over everyone, you are in for a big disappointment. But when the people you care for are sending you signals that there's room for improvement, you should receive these messages gratefully.

Figure 2.1. Brand YOU image worksheet.

RECENT FEEDBACK FROM FRIENDS AND FAMILY	SELF-ASSESSMENT TOOL	PERSONAL QUESTIONS TO POSE TO YOURSELF AND A TRUSTED FRIEND
[Simple comments may be a clue to their perception of your current image.]	[Jung-Myers-Briggs Typology, www.humanmetrics.com] [Myers-Briggs Foundation MBTI—Myers-Briggs Type Indicator] Plus many other self-help online questionnaires.	[See suggested questions]

JULIE'S IMAGE WORKSHEET

Remember Julie, from Chapter 1? Here's her worksheet for her brand image feedback. Figure 2.2 shows what Julie learned from questioning her friends and colleagues.

As has worked for Julie, finding your true brand image will help you better understand how you are perceived today by others.

Figure 2.2. Brand JULIE image worksheet.

RECENT FEEDBACK FROM FRIENDS AND FAMILY	SELF-ASSESSMENT TOOL ONLINE PERSONALITY TEST	PERSONAL QUESTIONS POSED TO YOURSELF AND A TRUSTED FRIEND
Family: → Mother is concerned about me, but happy I am out of the bad marriage. She is still very close, but worries about my future personally and professionally. → Brother John thinks I really missed the boat by not going to college and I have basically reaped what I have sown. → Father is no more than a birthday card and a quick visit during the Christmas season.	→ Julie learned that her personality is a: • Moderately expressed *extravert* • Slightly expressed *sensing personality* • *Moderately expressed* feeling personality • *Distinctly expressed* judging personality → As a person portrayed as a "Provider," Julie became aware of how much she was programmed to serve others. → No wonder I have never taken the time to "help myself." → It was also eye-opening to realize how sensitive I am to the feelings of others.	Self: → I am unsure of myself. → I question where I am in life. → Yet, I know I am good at what I do at work. → I rely on my technical knowledge of retailing and my store to prop up lagging areas of my life. → I remember my disdain for school but yearn to advance beyond my current level and recognize my limitations without a college degree → I am locked into the same group of friends, associated with the working world. Co-Workers and Customers: → Co-workers see me as a self-made woman. I started at the ground floor and am already a manager at age 28. I am always willing to help a co-worker and am viewed as a real leader. → Managers see me as a shining example of a person who has made it through dedication and hard work. "If only you had a college degree, you could really move up," shared one upper level manager. → Customers are always happy to me. I am so helpful that a customer said, "I come to this store partly because you work here."

Understanding your current brand image will be instructive when you begin to chart the path to your purposeful future.

Developing a new Brand YOU requires constant reinforcement and is more than just window dressing. Once you have a good understanding of where you currently stand, it is easier to begin creating a new identity (Brand YOU) that will be more fulfilling and that will lead to your very own repositioning effort. In the next chapter, we move on to brand identity.

CHAPTER 3

WHAT DO I WANT TO STAND FOR?

STEP THREE: DETERMINE YOUR BRAND
YOU *IDENTITY AND ESSENCE*

"The value of identity, of course, is that so often with it comes purpose."

—RICHARD R. GRANT

AS BRAND IMAGE REFERS to the current perception of your personal brand, think of *brand identity* as what you would like your personal brand to stand for in the future. Visualizing your desired Brand YOU identity requires a clear picture of your aspirations, strengths, and core values. Consistent with Grant's quote above, your personal identity can be a key component of unlocking your personal passion and inner drive. Or, in terms of personal branding, each of us can define and craft a vision of exactly what we want to stand for. That vision is our brand identity.

This vision of your future image will lead to your personal

positioning plan. Clarifying your unique identity is the starting point to developing that brand you would like to become. While being true to yourself, you will envision what you want to represent, based on the values and principles that are such an important part of your life. For example, rather than try to become your job at work, what if you tried to find the job that better matched your inner self? In other words, you will craft a self-description and then match it to a job description. That may seem backwards in accordance with the way things have typically been done, but it's quite logical. And the likelihood of happiness and success certainly improves when you know yourself before you choose your career path.

BUILDING YOUR OWN IDENTITY

You have great strengths that will help you grow to become all you should and could be. After all, *everyone*'s a work-in-progress. With that in mind, you can use your strengths as a conduit to personal fulfillment. These strengths are your personal equities, and they can be leveraged and transferred to different areas of professional development, to community service, and to personal satisfaction. How often have you been told to eliminate your weaknesses? While it is important to seek daily improvement, what if you instead took your strong points and put them to even greater use? In other words, why not aggressively and energetically focus on using your strong points, core competencies, and powerful assets to develop awesome, powerful, unique abilities and competencies? This type of thinking can unleash a powerful force for personal growth.

Building your own identity is grounded on the proposition that you have great strengths and that you are not yet all you should and could be.

In the business world, *brand equity* represents the value associated with a brand and is the sum of many building blocks that contribute to its strength. This equity reflects the economic evaluation of a brand in the marketplace or, in the case of personal branding, the recognized summation of your strengths and benefits. While brand equity can be quantified, or given a monetary value, for a corporate or product brand, that is less relevant when applied to a person. However, understanding the power of *personal equity* is an important step in building your brand identity. Brand equity is made up of many intangibles; the higher the brand equity, the more competitive advantage a brand will have in the marketplace. As the brand image and identity grow, generally speaking the brand equity also grows. A healthy brand identity contributes to strong brand equity, and vice versa. So, what equities do you have that can become an integral part of the identity you will create? Let's look at some examples.

The Coca-Cola Brand Identity

As a corporate example, The Coca-Cola Company has long been recognized as an organization with significant brand equity with over four hundred brands available in virtually every nook and cranny of the world. The flagship brand Coca-Cola soft drink has stood the test of time—over 120 years. In fact, Coca-Cola alone is

recognized as the most valuable brand in the world by the respected Interbrand Corporation. Valued at over US $67 billion, the Coca-Cola brand (Coke) has effectively become a part of modern world culture. Though its advertising campaigns have changed over the years, Coca-Cola ("The Real Thing") has always stood for a "real" cola drink with authenticity. This identity has been built over the decades with consistent values and differentiated elements. Many competitors have taken aim at Coke, but the brand continues to command number-one position globally in rankings of brand equity. After all, if you stand for "the real thing," every competitor is just an imitator.

Just as Coca-Cola has remained true to its time-tested identity, you have the same opportunity to stand for something that is equally relevant to you. This Brand YOU identity should reflect your own unique equities and core essence. This will ensure you create an identity that is meaningful and sustainable over the long term.

The Tiger Woods Brand Identity

Perhaps no one has ruled a sport and set such a completely new standard of extraordinary performance as has Tiger Woods. Tiger has maintained a laser-beam focus on perfecting his golf game, with unprecedented success. By 2007, Tiger had won thirteen major professional golf championships and an astounding 61 PGA Tour events. But even at the young age of 31 years, Tiger Woods had attained the achievement of being fifth on the list of all-time PGA tournament victories. Yet even with this phenomenal success, he seemingly remains discontent. Spending hours thinking and rethinking every shot, choice of club, every stance, and whatever else can be systematically improved, Woods is the mark of a true cham-

pion. Even after winning major golf tournaments, he chose to re-tool his golf swing, with his professional golf instructor at his side.

This extreme degree of focus defines Tiger's brand identity. When people are asked what they think of when they see a photograph of Woods, the responses are intriguing. They say that Tiger stands for perfection, winning, competitiveness, constant improvement, confidence, and intensity. For people, Woods never says never; he relentlessly pursues the best. In fact, rarely do people use the descriptor "golfer" when describing Tiger, inasmuch as that is what he does, not what he is. Yes, Tiger Woods is probably the best golfer in history, yet this is his functional product. The other descriptors represent the attributes of his strong brand identity and well-accepted brand image.

Woods's unique brand identity includes strong personal equities that could be transferred to other endeavors. It is no surprise that many consumer brands have struck deals with him. After his 21st birthday, in 1996, Woods started his endorsement of many different brands. Nike was one of the first companies to team up with Woods in a formal brand-building arrangement. This kind of endorsement represents a brilliant example of transferable equity: Woods brings Nike the attributes of a proven winner; Nike provides Tiger Woods with a medium in which to connect with millions of people who may be casual golfers, at best. Thus, every time a consumer puts on a Nike golf shirt or a pair of Nike golf shoes, he or she feels a little bit of the Tiger equity that comes with that Nike swoosh logo. The match between Nike and Tiger Woods is a winning formula because the parties share common values built around high performance.

And while Tiger is a fabulous golfer, he has created a brand identity that transcends the sport. He is now taking his quest for perfection into other walks of life. For example, he has established

the Tiger Woods Foundation, dedicated to helping disadvantaged children improve their lives. He also conducts golf clinics around the country. The Tiger Woods Learning Center is a 35,000-square-foot educational facility in Anaheim, California, for students between grades 4 and 12, that offers after-school and day programs.

Obviously, Tiger has taken his passion for golf excellence and high performance and developed them into a world-class strength that has helped him build a fulfilling life. What are your passions? What are your personal strengths, and how hard have you worked at developing these areas of your life? What can you learn from observing stellar brands like Tiger Woods?

THE BRAND YOU EQUITY CHART

You have equities, similar to Tiger Woods, that can be redirected to serve you better. Identifying your assets and liabilities has helped open your eyes to the possibilities that lie ahead of you. The Brand YOU equity chart (Figure 3.1) will now help you organize your personal balance sheet to discover your strengths as well as your gaps.

Realize that everyone has strengths and gaps. However, successful people have determined how to take these personal or professional strengths and build a rewarding situation that compensates for the gaps. Notice in the figure that you will identify gaps rather than weaknesses. A "weakness" sounds like some kind of defect or flaw. It's more productive to view these things as gaps or potential limitations. Gaps can be filled. Limitations can be improved upon.

Figure 3.1. Brand YOU equity table.

STRENGTHS	GAPS

Successful people have determined how to use personal or professional strengths to build a rewarding situation that compensates for any gaps.

Let's play this out and think about what it means to fill in the boxes provided. When you place items in the "Strengths" box, you should be thinking "I am skilled, strong, competent, and confident in these items. I need to accentuate the positive, promote these strengths, leverage these abilities, and use them to my advantage. I need to be careful not to overcompensate my basic gaps

with extraordinary strengths." Of course, when you add items to the "Gaps" box, you are admitting your areas of concern, which you should consider candidates for improvement.

As you construct your equity chart, think in terms of the personal, professional, community, spiritual, athletic, financial, and other parts of your life that deserve your time. A holistic inventory of your strengths and gaps can be eye-opening. If you are good at taking complex situations and sorting through the chaos, this is a unique strength that you should not underestimate. What if you determine you lack the ability to network with others? This is worthy of logging in the "Gaps" box.

Strengths

Imagine that you have a personal strength in the "gift of gab." In other words, you are a great conversationalist. Having this skill—this strength, this asset—you are able to strike up conversations with perfect strangers that result in quick connections. People genuinely enjoy talking with you because you listen carefully, respond with an inquisitive nature, and portray a genuine sense of curiosity. Now, let's say that, as a recent college graduate, you have a gap called "lack of business experience." You have time on your hands and a desire to build your new identity in the world of retail sales and merchandising.

Remember your "gift of gab" strength? What if you found a place to volunteer or to "work" where the job requires providing helpful information to customers? For example, every mall has an information station to assist shoppers. This might be just the chance for you to relaunch the Brand YOU. The beautiful thing about this is that you're now busy, active, productive, and doing something you do well (i.e., communicating), and something you

truly enjoy (i.e., interacting with people). You are also putting yourself into an environment where you can build your network.

"Strengths" represent areas of success, pride, skill, and anything else that you do well. These are capabilities you have developed over time and may now come naturally to you. In fact, strengths may be what are called out when you, as well as others, describe who you are. You are so skilled in these areas that you may be seen as a teacher. These strengths are part of your identity and definitely are your assets. Perhaps you're compassionate, or highly analytical, or high-energy, or a great writer, or work well with senior citizens, or are an expert in a field of business, or are a great athlete. We all have a number of strengths. A key to happiness is matching those strengths and competencies with activities you are passionate about. As an example, wouldn't it be wonderful for a woman who loves working with children, and who is competent, to own, operate, or manage a children's day-care center? Now, that's a great match!

Sometimes strengths are overdeveloped, to the point that they can hinder further growth and development. In fact, there are times when people use their strengths to compensate for a gap. Just be cautious not to overcompensate in order to hide weakness. Also, you don't want to spend so much time working to correct a weakness that you end up diminishing your strengths. Consider, for example, a high school baseball player who is a gifted batter. He is able to hit several home runs during batting practice every day before a game. After practice, this player is often in the batting cage, hitting extra balls to further hone his strength. People talk about his ability to "hit the long ball"; in fact, his dream is to earn a baseball scholarship to college. Now, unfortunately, he is operating with a blind spot. While he has chosen to overdevelop his batting strength, he has not mastered the fielding skills required of a

reliable first baseman. Unless he improves his catching and throwing skills, he likely won't even continue to be a starter, much less earn a scholarship.

The question is, What strengths do you use to overcompensate for basic gaps? Do you avoid correcting a few essential gaps because you think you can muscle through them with your strengths? If so, you may be astounded just how far a little effort can go in working on closing gaps. Filling in the chart will help you see your strengths to deliver within the normal expectations rather than overtaxing these areas. Remember, focusing on improving your gaps as well as improving your strengths requires a balanced approach to activity and practice.

Gaps

Gaps are areas that could represent potential barriers if left unresolved. Notice that gaps may not be actual weaknesses, unless they get in the way of building your new Brand YOU. These holes have the potential to become priorities for personal attention, deserving specific action plans. For example, if you are an expert in the area of teaching, yet you are unskilled in the newest technologies used in teaching, this is a true gap. It is possible that your career as a teacher will be limited unless you learn these new technologies. In fact, it may very well be this gap that prevents you from progressing to the next level of your career and the best part of your life. Therefore, enhancing your computer skills may become a personal priority if you are to be seen as a contemporary teacher, in tune with today's students.

Sometimes people choose to either overlook a gap or avoid dealing with it, reverting to outright denial mode. Any gap that is neglected has the prospect of growing and becoming an issue, or

declining and never being a problem. That is important to understand. You should not feel the obligation to become "gapless." In fact, this is the beauty of thinking of yourself as a brand. Remember, a brand is focused, targeted, and does not try to be all things to all people. This view of yourself gives you the license to live with gaps and be self-actualized. You may find that some gaps represent significant upside potential if they could be minimized or eliminated. Other gaps have absolutely no bearing on where you want to take your new Brand YOU. Nevertheless, it is worthwhile to be aware of the gaps so you can contain future problems if they arise.

Picture a scene in which a homemaker has been happily married for twenty years and has reared two children who are preparing to leave for college. She is now beginning to think about life as an empty-nester, with her husband still gainfully employed. Early in her marriage, she worked as an accountant, but with handling all the family responsibilities, she hasn't worked for over fifteen years. So much has changed; she wants to get back into the workforce, yet she is filled with doubts driven by what she senses are her gaps. She doesn't believe she is contemporary in her grasp of the world out there now.

She is most concerned about her confusion of where to begin. This could become the paralyzing question that constrains her desires. But rather than consider this an insurmountable gap, she takes one small step by calling her church to see if there is a support group for women like her. Lo and behold, there is a group that meets twice a month to discuss the job market and to assist people who plan on reentering the workforce. One thing leads to another, and she is connected with a church member who operates an employment agency, with contacts in the accounting world. Believe it or not, these small but important steps are critical in beginning to

deal with personal gaps. In this case, the woman needed to close this gap in order to achieve her goal.

DISCOVERING YOUR LIKES AND DISLIKES

Frequently, people develop a skill or strength in an area in which they have little interest or passion pursuing. How many times have you realized that you are quite good at something you actually dislike? This is especially true in the working world. If you are a great "numbers person" at work, your manager may take it for granted that you enjoy this activity. The better you are at the analytical work, the more assignments land on your desk. But being good at something doesn't necessarily mean you love that something you're good at. This becomes a self-fulfilling prophecy, in a reverse sort of way. If this is a real dislike and you strongly desire to be in another area, you very well could move into a precarious win-lose situation. While it is a win for your employer that you work with numbers, it is a losing proposition for you.

Likes are those things that really excite you and you are happy when you are doing them. Whenever you have free time, it is a good bet you try to do these things. You may want to introduce others to the activities, whether it is fly fishing, stamp collecting, visiting fine art galleries, or strolling through antique centers. Frequently, these personal enjoyments become serious hobbies, which then pay the dividend of introducing you to people with similar interests. You may like putting together an ornate scrapbook that helps you relive that special vacation trip you made to Hawaii.

Whatever your likes, try to spend more time engaged in these

activities because they provide fun for you. They're easy, they're fulfilling, they make you smile. In the true spirit of "living the life you've imagined," wouldn't it be terrific to find a job for which people actually pay you to do what you love to do? On the wall of Baseball Hall of Fame manager Tommy Lasorda, in his office at Dodger Stadium in Los Angeles, there's a sign that showcases a quote from inspirational writer Harvey Mackay: "Find something you love to do and you'll never have to work a day in your life."

Dislikes are those activities or situations that you find distasteful, unexciting, unsatisfying, or any other "dis" words that come to mind. You hate doing these things, and frankly nobody is going to change your feelings. Face it, everybody has something they just do not enjoy doing. You may have tried many different times, and in many different ways, but for whatever reason they are just not your thing.

Now, do not become confused. There are tasks you dislike that you still need to accomplish. Students may not like doing homework, but in order to graduate, they must complete their studies. A talented cook, who takes pleasure in preparing gourmet meals, may not enjoy washing the pots and pans. You will be able to discern between those tasks that must be done and the habitual things that you can eliminate because they become distasteful over time. If you are an optimistic person, who looks on the bright side of life, yet you find you are spending an inordinate amount of time with "friends" who constantly complain and are negative, this is a dislike staring you in the face. Remaining in this zone of grumbling and whining is an act you can opt out of, or at least reduce.

Many people love traveling to exotic places. They spend weeks or months researching their next great destination, the methods of travel, places to stay, and things to do once they arrive. Yet others

cringe at the mere thought of airport security, a long flight peppered with delays, crowds, undependable ground transportation, and anything else that can go wrong when you leave home. In fact, they are unimpressed with the globetrotting stories shared at neighborhood gatherings and are satisfied with something as simple as a 30-minute walk in the nearby nature preserve. This diversity of outlook is what makes the world go around. Everyone recognizes that there are things they do not enjoy doing, and in these instances, it is fine to avoid those situations. Of course, this assumes you are not employed as a travel agent, which requires regular travel. If so, you've made a bad career choice. Can you imagine a pediatrician who doesn't like children?

As you consider your strengths and gaps, take some time also to ask yourself some fundamental questions about your likes and dislikes. Of the elements in your brand equity chart, which do you truly like and which do you dislike? Remember, there is a correlation between superior performance and enjoying what you do for a living. Passion is an important part of success. Your Brand YOU deserves better than mere accommodation. Yes, you must mix the good with the bad, and a balanced life includes plenty of both. However, beware if you are good at something yet dislike everything about this activity.

If you are a great bartender and have been tending bar for several years, and you earn good wages and tips, but you hate the hours, the smoke-filled environment, the same old people, and never having a night off, you are out of balance. Even if you're making terrific money, you're paying too high a price for this financial success. Maybe you can leverage your strengths in a different field. What if you were to take your extensive knowledge of that business and work as a manufacturer's representative who sells beverages and spirits to local bars and taverns? This is what the process is

meant to show you. Are you positioned where you would like to be? Or is there a better place for your personal brand?

Many of the attributes you have listed in your chart can be flexed into new and rewarding activities and vocations. The numbers person mentioned earlier may never be able to transfer to another department within her own company; yet, she can take steps to alter her brand identity so as to become a viable candidate with a different employer that is a better match with her passions. Frequently, you can even reset your identity with your current employer; however, it may be easier to investigate employment with another firm, especially if you want to break away from a deeply ingrained brand image. Having strong personal equity in the financial area would be an attractive skill for any company that serves customers in this industry. Indeed, in this high-growth industry, a numbers person could move into almost any area of greater professional interest.

Time is your most valuable asset, yet time is finite. There are only so many hours in the day and so many days in the week. Whether you spend 80 percent of your time doing what you like or 80 percent doing what you dislike, there are still only 24 hours in a day. Optimize your time spent on necessary tasks that you may dislike, such as homework, and minimize your time spent on unnecessary dislikes. That way you can maximize your time doing your desired likes. By giving your seesaw of likes and dislikes a more favorable balance, you can materially improve your attitude and become a more fulfilled Brand YOU, as well as a happier person.

The Brand YOU Time Balance Grid

Later in this book you will become aware that, regardless of who you are and what you do, you have a job description. This notion of

job description will be further developed in the next chapter. For now, realize that whether you are a volunteer at the local library, a stay-at-home dad, or a young executive, you spend a majority of time doing what is generally termed your job description. So, in accordance with what we've just said about likes and dislikes, you need to examine how you spend your time, so that you can better achieve the balance we've discussed. The Brand YOU time balance grid will help (see Figure 3.2).

For this exercise, fill in the estimated number of hours you spend in each category during an average week. Remember, "Job Time" represents your area of primary responsibility. For example, if you are a full-time college student, this is your job time and it takes up a major block of your calendar. "Chore Time" represents the amount of time you spend doing routine activities. This could be mowing the lawn or going to the store. "Obligation Time" corresponds to the commitments you have made to friends, family, or community. Finally, anything that does not fit the first three categories should be classified as "Other Time." Try to be as specific as you can when allocating the number of hours. And remember also that each week begins with only 168 total hours; when you take out 56 hours for the recommended 8 hours of sleep each night, or just rest and relaxation, your total hours available are only 112 per week. For each category, divide the total number of hours per week by 112 to see what percentage of waking hours you are spending in the various grids.

The grid shows how much time you are spending in activities you like and dislike. It also helps you identify which time is spent doing activities you believe are required and those that may be voluntary. After all, some hours are spent doing things that must get done, but there are other activities you should question, as you are trying to free up time for more rewarding things.

AVERAGE WEEK	JOB TIME	CHORE TIME	OBLIGATION TIME	OTHER TIME	% OF AVAILABLE TIME
Activities required and you like					
Activities not required and you like					
Activities required and you dislike					
Activities not required and you dislike					
Total number of hours					
% of your available time ($\frac{total\ hours}{112}$)					

Figure 3.2. Brand YOU time balance grid.

For example, suppose you spend 15 hours per week in the "Obligation Time"—"Activities not required and you dislike" box. This time is shared among various activities, predominantly on the weekend, that have begun to feel more like chores than obligations. Well, this is over 13 percent of your total available time, and that eats up your valuable weekend time. What if you shifted just 10 of those hours of unrequired "dislike" activities to 10 hours of worthwhile "like" activities? This could make a huge difference in building your new Brand YOU. It will also identify some unproductive time that could be reallocated to working on filling one of those gaps you have discovered. This view that you can rebalance your time beginning immediately will set you free to focus your energy on more positive efforts.

SOME EXAMPLES OF REBUILT BRAND IDENTITIES

You may believe that your brand image (the current outsider perceptions of your personal brand) is a barrier to your continued personal development. Before you throw in the towel, consider rebuilding your brand identity (what you want your personal brand to stand for). Let's look at how some others have done that very thing.

Martha Stewart Turns Around

Someone who had built a successful business, and lifestyle, around her delight with home furnishings and domestic ac-

tivities, Martha Stewart is a classic example of someone who experienced a major brand image meltdown but who has rebounded with a stronger brand identity. As the leading "domestic diva" in the United States, Martha Stewart established a broad-based firm, Martha Stewart Living Omnimedia, to manage her television, print, and merchandising empire. As Chairwoman and Chief Executive Officer, Stewart led the company to a public stock offering on the New York Stock Exchange. The stock rallied from an initial price of $18 per share to $38 by the end of day one. Martha Stewart had built a brand identity that reflected her commitment to her brand essence. She demonstrated her abilities as a keen business leader, publisher, television star, and socialite. By doing exactly what she loved, and was very good at, she had established a multibillion-dollar business that allowed her to leverage her personal strengths.

Suddenly, in 2002, her identity was shattered with allegations of insider trading of the ImClone stock, an allegation made worse by her lying under oath to federal investigators. Stewart was convicted in March 2004 for obstruction of justice. Instead of pursuing numerous appeals, Martha Stewart started to serve her five-month sentence in a federal prison.

During her time at Alderson Federal Prison Camp in West Virginia, Martha Stewart befriended many prisoners and carried on her zeal for cooking, and even daily housekeeping activities. Upon her release from prison, she reconnected with her image and her consumer base with an accountability that has contributed positively to her brand identity. Now, this is not meant to disregard her crime, but you have to admire her ability to turn a difficult situation into a positive one. She relied on her core equities and essence to rebuild her brand identity. Martha Stewart continues to build

her brand in an authentic way, and has used this experience to positively influence her life.

L.L. Bean Puts Its Brand on a Car

Another way of building your identity is to take your personal strengths to nontraditional places. These clever synergies can result in some surprising success stories for you, as they have for L.L. Bean, the mail-order retailer.

L.L. Bean is a well-recognized American clothing and outdoor equipment company, founded in 1912. Beginning with unique waterproof boots, L.L. Bean developed a reputation as a respected clothier and accessories leader catering to active people with an affinity for the outdoors.. With an array of catalogues blanketing almost every home, this company has expanded into a huge retailer with a line that goes far beyond its initial "outdoors" image.

But that was not enough for L.L. Bean. Subaru, a Japanese automotive company, is well known for its all-wheel drive vehicles that are as comfortable on a city street as off the road. With only a few models, Subaru is one of the perennial winners in the annual *Consumer Reports* ratings games, especially in terms of reliability and value for money. Both of these companies recognized the power of combining their brand equities by co-branding and producing the collaborative, limited edition L.L. Bean Subaru Outback. On the surface, a mail-order company and a car company seem a strange fit. However, by recognizing the transferable equities and staying true to the essence of both brands, a unique product emerged with dual brand power. Both of these companies have become lifestyle brands. Individuals are capable of co-branding as well, aligning themselves with others for mutual benefit.

THE IMPORTANCE OF BRAND ESSENCE

When we use the word *essence* we're trying to describe the most basic nature of something. A substance's essence does not change over time, and its appeal is not driven by fad. It is considered authentic, reflective of a core belief system or set of principles. When applied to brands, *essence* is its very heart and soul. Recognizing and understanding a brand's essence is a vital part of building a successful brand. That which is real, is tangible and sustainable with respect to a brand, is the driving force for all future brand development.

Your *brand essence* includes, but is not limited to, your background, your lifestyle, your language patterns, your philosophy of life, your views on right and wrong, the expressions you use, the stores you frequent, the kinds of foods you eat, the clothes you wear, your unique experiences, your special areas of expertise, your gifts to others, the things others respect about you, the people you respect, your reliability, your wit and wisdom, and so on. Some aspects of your brand essence are worthy of praise and respect; others need work. Brands, even personal brands, are always works-in-progress, as we've mentioned before.

Example: The Starbucks Brand Essence

In 1987, Howard Schulz, a marketing executive with Starbucks, organized a group of investors and purchased this company. Any market analyst might have thought this was a poor move, since the coffee market was allegedly saturated and characterized by commodity-priced cans of coffee in local retailers. Also, the standard coffee fare in our nation's grocery outlets was what's called

"soluble coffee," or what we call instant coffee. Schulz, having admired the old tradition of the Italian coffee bar and café, visualized a Starbucks brand essence that has resulted in global expansion and a powerful iconic brand. Where soluble coffee is attached to no experience, Starbucks' positioning is all experiential.

Starbucks views its business as one cup at a time, not a mass marketer. With very little formal advertising, Starbucks relies on its ability to deliver its brand essence, which results in favorable word of mouth and drives customer brand loyalty. Landor Associates describes this very well: "Anyone can copy the coffee shop and décor. But the essence of Starbucks is not about the coffee, although it's great coffee. It's about the coffee-drinking and the coffeehouse experience." This experiential aspect of Starbucks helps people feel welcome and connected to a broader social community.

Starbucks has created an emotional bond with millions of consumers. In offering a product that goes well beyond the basic cup of coffee, this firm has built a lasting relationship that has reinvented the coffee arena. This has been accomplished through a growth strategy built on executing the brand essence on the corners of streets all around the world. This brand essence continues to be the key to maintaining brand-loyal consumers. In spite of the fact that an estimated 70 percent of the coffee sales is for on-the-go consumers, these people still take a few minutes to come inside a Starbucks, inhale the coffee aroma, have their special coffee crafted by baristas, and return ready to face the world. This is quite a tribute in today's hustle and bustle world—that so many people will take the time to stop, park, get out of their car, and go inside for a cup of experience. And this doesn't include all the people in cities, who duck into the corner Starbucks before the theater in the evening, the stu-

dents who use it as a study room, and the workers who prefer it to the office coffee wagon.

Over the past few years, Starbucks has grown its outlet base at an exceptional pace and has begun to experience deterioration in some of the core values that made this brand so strong. The growth rate of sales at stores open for more than a year has slowed dramatically, and new competitors are entering the coffee arena. In fact, after stepping aside, Howard Shulz has returned as CEO to try to reinvigorate this brand to the essence that made it so strong. Only time will tell if Starbucks continues to deliver a consumer proposition that is consistent with its original brand essence.

Another example of an organization that was founded and developed with a strong brand essence is The Body Shop.

Example: The Body Shop

In 1976, The Body Shop was founded in the UK by Dame Anita Roddick. Roddick, a self-proclaimed activist, started her business as a single store operation in order to create a source of income for herself and her two daughters as her husband was traveling across the Americas. This child of Italian immigrants grew up as an outcast and admired the likes of James Dean. By the time she turned 10, after finding a book on the Holocaust, she had a growing discontent with social injustice. This inner passion lives with her today. She became a teacher, traveled the world, met her husband Gordon, and opened a restaurant, followed by a hotel in her birth town of Littlehampton. She was able to quickly learn the business of buying and selling for profit in spite of no formal training in the retail trade. Today, The Body Shop has over 2,100

stores that do business in 55 countries, and offers a product assortment of over 1,200 items.

Her brand essence comes through loud and clear in the principles of The Body Shop. While this global organization is in the business of manufacturing and selling cosmetics products, it is differentiated by its five values: Protect the Planet, Support Community Trade, Defend Against Animal Testing, Defend Human Rights, and Build Self-Esteem. These five values act as a roadmap for everything the company does. Whether it is the development of a new lotion or the carbon footprint each piece of packaging creates, The Body Shop is focused on delivering profits with a greater purpose.

So, how do these values come to life in actual operations? The company's purchasing procedures exclude any ingredients that use animals in cosmetic testing since December 31, 1990. Additionally, the company has selected Stop Violence in the Home as their commitment to defend human rights and activate self-esteem. It has also developed its own charity, The Body Shop Foundation, which began in 1990. This foundation provides financial assistance to startups and economically starved organizations in the areas of human and civil rights and environmental and animal protection. Obviously, this foundation serves the community trade and is aligned with the values of the company.

Dame Anita Roddick, a social rebel with a purpose, has found a way to combine her passion for activism with a cosmetics and beauty business that has a distinct moral compass. This strategy has paid off financially for the organization, which delivered revenue for fiscal year 2006 of 485.6 million British pounds and total net income of 29.2 million British pounds. So, not only does this company represent a moral compass, but it also delivers significant profits to its corporation.

YOUR BRAND ESSENCE

Your Brand YOU also has a brand essence. Having just identified your brand equities, you should better understand those strengths that are within you and have the potential for transferability. You should also recognize how certain experiences in your life have had a disproportionately high impact. Regardless of the situation or occurrence, you have now chronicled these within your five life phases, during your Brand YOU audit. Isn't it interesting how powerful a few years can be in influencing your current life? Why should you allow a situation that happened in high school have such a grip on your life today? Yet, this is exactly what so many people allow to happen. They choose to let their history control their future. You, however, have the opportunity to create a future that leverages who you really are and unleash your brand essence.

Consider your brand essence as the true north on your life's compass. Within you are the values, principles, and beliefs that guide your life. When your actions are in sync with this essence, you are being true to yourself and are probably achieving your personal goals. But living a life that is inconsistent with your brand essence is a recipe for conflict, confusion, disappointment, and challenge. It is also a recipe for failure. It is unfair to yourself, as well as to those around you, for you to live in contradiction with your inner essence.

Finding your brand essence might be the most powerful concept in this book. Recall a time when you were doing something that you truly loved. You garnered immense joy and pleasure from this moment, and you could not wait to do it again. You may even feel a special call to give of your time in this activity. This feeling symbolizes what drives you deep inside and is representative of your values and principles.

99

An easy way to unlock these doors to your brand essence is to describe the things that you really like doing and the things that you definitely dislike doing. That's exactly what you've done earlier in this chapter, with the Brand YOU equity chart and the Brand YOU time balance grid. When you are doing something that you love and you are very good at, the chances for your new Brand YOU to succeed are huge. So, you've determined your likes and dislikes; now, it's time to sort through the likes and discover which you feel truly passionate about. It's a known fact that many things will catch your eye, but only a limited few will catch your heart. *Passion points* define the things that catch your heart and that you find rewarding.

Certainly, many people are passionate about everything from gardening to sporting events. So, what are you passionate about? Do you have any real passions? If not, this is reason for personal exploration. Make it your business to find what you can become—what you can be passionate about. This is vital. Author T. Alan Armstrong wrote, "If there is no passion in your life, then have you really lived? Find your passion, whatever it may be. Become it, and let it become you and you will find great things happen FOR you, TO you and BECAUSE of you."

The Brand YOU Essence Map

Figure 3.3 is a useful matrix for mapping your brand essence. Separated into four quadrants, this map will help you plot your passion points and areas of personal satisfaction. The purpose of this map is to bring 20-20 vision to what is inside you and to encourage you to let your potential loose and gain insight into your interests and passions. Anything that is mapped into the upper right quadrant of the Brand YOU essence map is a personal pas-

Figure 3.3. Brand YOU essence map.

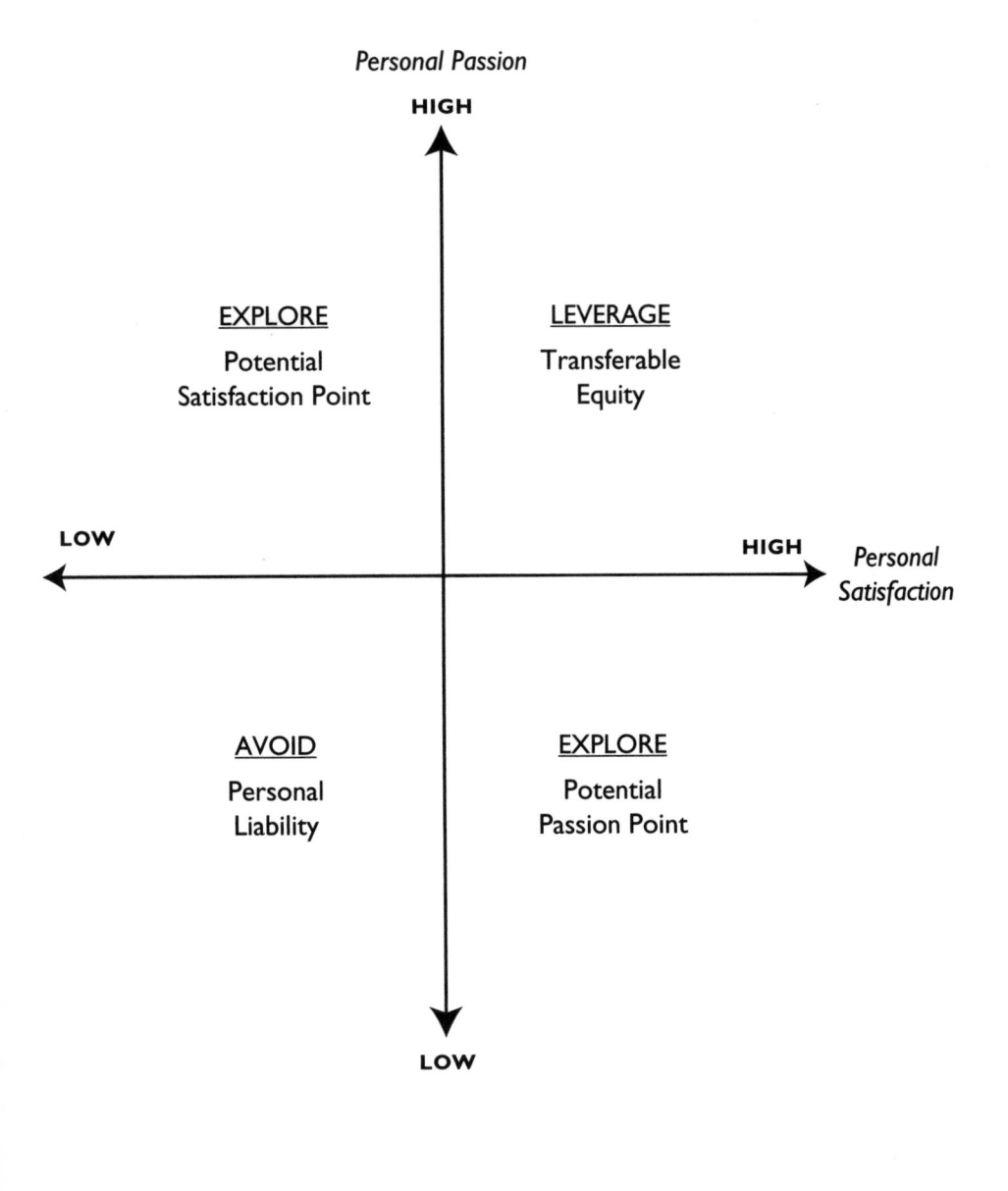

Personal Passion

HIGH

EXPLORE
Potential
Satisfaction Point

LEVERAGE
Transferable
Equity

LOW

HIGH *Personal
Satisfaction*

AVOID
Personal
Liability

EXPLORE
Potential
Passion Point

LOW

sion that brings you great satisfaction and can be leveraged to improve your life.

➤ *Upper left quadrant:* This sector is interesting for you to explore because, with a little work, you may be able to grow your level of satisfaction here. For example, this satisfaction level may be driven by a skill gap that you can develop. Given your high level of passion, it is a shame not to at least consider this where you can increase your satisfaction.

➤ *Lower right quadrant:* This sector represents potential, since these are situations that compel a high level of satisfaction. Is it possible that you could have more passion for these activities if you knew more about them? Low passion levels can easily be heightened when you derive greater satisfaction from the activities.

➤ *Lower left quadrant:* Stay away from this sector. These are things that you do not like doing, you have no passion for doing, and that do not motivate you. Avoid these activities because they represent your *anti-essence*.

➤ *Upper right quadrant:* This sector includes activities that you can turn to for personal satisfaction. For example, a working mother who cares for her three children might want a reprieve each week. She determines that this desire for private time is a nagging gap in her life. Because she accepts her responsibility as a mother, she finds that a one-hour soak in a hot tub, with the door shut and with quiet music playing and scented candles nearby, is just the escape that brings her great personal satisfaction while optimizing her passion for meditation. Believe it or not, the process can be this simple. What change will help you find your brand essence?

Understanding your equities and brand essence is liberating. Think of how free you will feel when you know your guiding

principles in life. You'll recognize what you really stand for, and what brand image you want others to have about you. By merging your brand equities with your brand essence, you will create a powerful new Brand YOU. You will also be surprised to learn just how many transferable equities you have at your disposal.

Why is this step so important in the personal branding process? Simply put, to place yourself in the satisfying and successful life that you imagine, you need to find your inner drive and to discover the skills you have that can help you find your best space. Having a brand identity that is right for you is no accident. It begins with looking deep inside yourself to find out what motivates you and to discover the principles that guide your life. And it is equally important to recognize where you do not want to be, as it is to visualize where you do want to be. The Brand YOU Essence Map will help you capture the magic that exists at the intersection of brand essence and brand equity, and is key to opening the door to a new Brand YOU.

JULIE'S BRAND ESSENCE

Remember Julie? Let's take a look at her results from having filled in the three charts in this chapter. When we left off last time, Julie had decided to take her personal observations and feedback from friends to the next level. She began by stepping back and looking at her life to date. Julie reviewed her brand audit, which brought to the surface some old problems that she had not dealt with before. Julie was beginning to realize that, while she felt somewhat destitute earlier, she was more upbeat about the good things she had accomplished. After all, her co-workers have respect

for her, and so do her customers. She is skilled at retail and is successfully living on her own. While her marriage had failed, she began to realize what courage it took to get out of that bad relationship. So, as she began to work on her brand identity, she filled out the Brand JULIE equity table (Figure 3.4).

Julie was beginning to see her important strengths, yet also some gaps appear. She was pleased to have identified some tangible areas of personal strength, and her gaps seemed manageable. Next, she decomposed her average week, using the Brand JULIE time balance grid in Figure 3.5.

Julie was unable to account for 26 percent of her time. This seemed to get lost in sitting around her apartment in the morning, having coffee and watching television. Clearly, Julie was alarmed

Figure 3.4. Brand JULIE equity table.

STRENGTHS	GAPS
• Success in retailing, including managing a department and working with others • Living on her own • Responsibility • Committed to a better life • Open-mindedness • Willing to try new things • Small, but loyal group of friends • Helping customers (people) • Eternal optimist • Friendships and trusting relationship with her mother	• High school diploma (where college is a requirement to move up) • Experience outside of retail • Somewhat isolated from other outside activities or opportunities • Life in a rut • Financially limited (basically living from paycheck to paycheck)

Figure 3.5. Brand JULIE time balance grid (average week).

AVERAGE WEEK	JOB TIME	CHORE TIME	OBLIGATION TIME	OTHER TIME	% OF AVAILABLE TIME
Activities required and you like	25 Working with customers	10 Grocery shopping and cooking			35 hours 31%
Activities not required and you like	5 Mentoring new co-workers		3 Speaking with Mother on phone	3—Exercise 2—Reading newspaper	13 hours 12%
Activities required and you dislike	10 Paperwork and register close-out process	10—Grabbing food on the run after working late 3—Laundry			23 hours 21%
Activities not required and you dislike	10 Daily commute by car of one hour each way		2 Weekend time with same old friends, having coffee		12 hours 11%
Total number of hours	50	23	5	5	83 hours
% of your available time $\left(\frac{\text{total hours}}{112}\right)$	45%	21%	4%	4%	74%

by this quick, easy, and troubling snapshot of her average and un-eventful life. The saving grace was that the 25 hours she spent with customers were enjoyable and within her job description. This observation is something she can build on while moving onto her re-branding plan.

Now, Julie mapped her passion points. By incorporating the information from the essence map (see Figure 3.6), she was able to get a clearer picture of her brand identity. So, here's her brand JULIE essence map.

While Julie knew she had more work to do to identify her new Brand JULIE identity, she was beginning to get a clear picture of what her strengths, gaps, passion points, and satisfaction drivers were. These insights were equally interesting when she completed her time balance grid. Merely understanding where all of her time was going and what made her happiest already felt very empowering. Now, Julie's resolve was mounting as she realized it was time to commit to a personal brand reinvention. Equipped with this helpful brand identity guidance, she prepared to move to her next phase of discovery and change.

Creative visualization is the process of just relaxing and seeing in your mind the way something will look or the way some activity will play out before it actually happens. It is important for everyone on a brand reinvention journey to give lots of time to thinking, What I want to stand for. Creatively visualize what that position will look like and even the reactions of others when they see a newly positioned Brand YOU. In some ways, defining your identity is also defining the endgame, the Brand YOU that you are aspiring to become.

You're making progress. Keep up the great work, and move on to the next step!

Figure 3.6. Brand JULIE essence map.

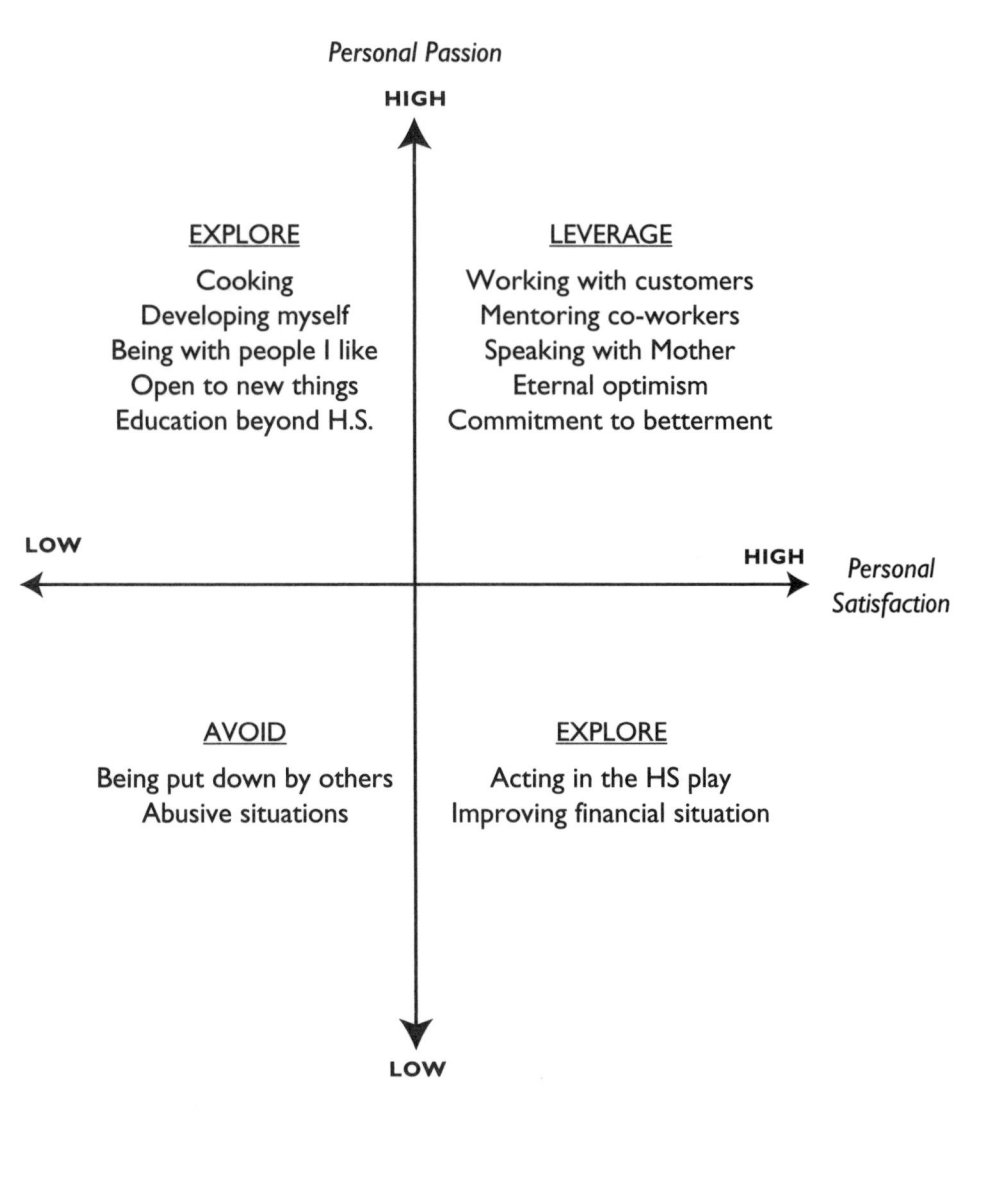

CHAPTER 4

I CAN GET THERE FROM HERE!

STEP FOUR: POSITION YOUR NEW BRAND **YOU**

"Trust yourself. You know more than you think you do."
—BENJAMIN SPOCK, 1946

WHAT IS *BRAND POSITIONING?* How do companies successfully position brands with consumers? And—what's important here—how can you position your new Brand YOU? Brand positioning could very well be a topic for an entire book itself.

Consumer goods companies like General Mills, Hanes, and Kraft General Foods give tremendous time and resources to this aspect of marketing. By the time a company gets to the pinpoint work of positioning its brand, much has already been done. The work of brand positioning always begins and ends with the consumer. What do the prospective consumers (end users) expect? And are there any unmet needs in the minds of these customers? To answer these questions, companies conduct exhaustive consumer segmentation analyses.

This type of analysis splits buyers into groups by their ethnicity, user habits, geography, socioeconomic level, per capita spending patterns, and so on. Words like *demographics, psychographics,* and *sociographics* are bantered about in marketing discussions because positioning is more science than art today. The effort is made to identify a precise group of customers that the brand will "go after" or "target," and then to map the programs that will reach these targets. These people become known to the marketers as the *target consumers.*

AN OVERVIEW OF THE POSITIONING PROCESS

The insights gained and decisions made as a result of these analyses begin the positioning work, which starts with a vivid description of the brand objectives and strategies. Carrying out these strategies constitutes the marketplace execution, which is then followed by constant monitoring and adjustments based on what is learned from consumer buying habits. In fact, the brand's positioning could very well be changed many times until the exact right—successful—program is in place. Think of it as a wheel that keeps revolving until the right position is found; this is the strategy that comprises the 7 Steps to Creating Your Most Successful Self, as shown in Figure 4.1.

Just as a corporate brand is a collection of perceptions in the mind of consumers, your personal brand relies on a similar collection of perceptions. "What do they think, what do they believe about *me*?" Great brands understand the end user very well and provide a unique benefit that meets or exceeds their needs. So,

Figure 4.1. The cycle of brand positioning.

1. Consumer Insights

2. Consumer Segmentation

3. Target Consumers

4. Competitive Analysis and Reality SWOT

5. Brand Positioning Statement

6. Objectives, Strategies

7. Marketplace Execution

8. Monitor and Adjust based on Consumer Learning

Great Positioning Creates Brand Insistence

companies try to "position" their brands within a specific area in the minds of consumers. Brand positioning is a mixture of art and science that results in a competitive advantage when compared with other options.

It is important to recognize that brand positioning happens whether companies choose to be proactive or not. In other

words, if a company pays no real attention to the space its brands occupy, then it will have abdicated the positioning job and relegated its space in the marketplace to chance (or the consumer) and possibly worse, to its competitors. In summary, positioning results in a credible and unique image of the product in the minds of customers. It communicates a promise that is delivered through actual experience. So, doesn't it make sense to use this same technique to establish a new personal brand identity that will capture and captivate its target as well?

Brands that follow this process are committed to occupying a unique, differentiated position, or space, in the marketplace. Those targeted spaces are a result of fact-based decisions and pragmatic approach, similar to the way you must define the space you want your personal brand to occupy. If you are successful, you will be a well-positioned brand in the eyes of your target audience, and you will command higher price points and enjoy "brand insistence."

Yes, you, too, can achieve higher levels of recognition, responsibility, and respect by building a well-positioned Brand YOU. Successful brands establish an emotional bond with the consumer that is stronger than merely the practical, that offers more than the on-the-surface benefits. Successful brands touch people's emotions and tap into their deepest values. Likewise, your personal brand can establish emotional bonds that will serve you well into the future.

Successful brands establish an emotional bond
that is stronger than merely the practical.
Successful brands touch people's emotions
and tap into their deepest values.

Indeed, this is how you want your new Brand YOU to be viewed by your targeted public. Through positioning you place the brand in a position that you will own, that will differentiate you. Companies want their brands to occupy the most valuable real estate in the world—a corner in the consumer's mind. In the case of personal branding, you want to occupy a similarly important spot of real estate in the minds of your own target audience.

What space do you want to occupy in the minds and hearts of others? Do you want to create a unique identity that reflects what you stand for, or would you prefer to just hope that others will sense your strengths and understand you? Or, even worse, do you want to settle for whatever happens to come your way? Settling is what most people do. They sit on the sideline, going through the motions of life that materialized around them, with neither rhyme nor reason to their decisions, if they even make any decisions. Fortunately, by reading this book, you have already made the decision to take control of your life and build a meaningful future for yourself.

POSITIONING A NEW BRAND YOU

Remember, what space do you want to occupy in the minds and hearts of others? Keep this question in mind as you move into the excitement of seeing, in your mind's eye, what your new Brand YOU will be like through positioning.

You should now begin to appreciate the importance of your work up to this point. You have already taken valuable time to step back and assess your personal situation. Up to this point, the focus of your reflection has been on your background and personal history. By examining your many experiences, both good and not

so good, you are ready to begin connecting the dots in your life. For example, how well have you dealt with those challenging situations in your past? Do you believe every day presents a fresh start, or do you carry the problems from yesterday into every day that follows? Have you begun to recognize the extraordinary learning that life's experiences have provided? What patterns do you see that you would like to develop further now? In short, what have you learned? What have you imagined for the future?

Your brand audit helped you realize that you are a function today of the life you have led so far. You have identified positive and negative experiences that you can carry forward with great benefit. After all, the key to life is to leverage the good, the bad, and the ugly of your life to move forward to a better future.

Ultimately, your brand image becomes your scorecard showing how well your positioning strategy is working. It is your litmus test for the positioning work. But first, your positioning work will allow you to determine what kind of identity you plan to establish and how best to communicate this to others. Given who you are, where do you want to go from here? After all, you have a bright future if you paint a picture that is inspirational and true to yourself. There is always a future for those who plan for it, and positioning will get you there.

Brand image is the scorecard showing how well your positioning strategy is working.

Let's take an example. Perhaps during your brand audit, you recognized that you were an avid gardener as a young adult, and

this gave you great pride. You reflected on the reputation you built, in having the finest garden in the neighborhood. Unfortunately, lately you have not had the time to devote to this activity, even though there are many times when you think about gardening and the joys it provided.

At the same time, you know that you have had a solid career and have reached a respectable level of responsibility in your company. Yet two specific opportunities surfaced during your audit. You've determined that you would like to develop a life outside and beyond your day-to-day employment. You also have recognized a personal desire to enhance your public-speaking skills in order to advance at work. But as a teenager in high school, your class presentation bombed. You were a bit of a joke to your classmates; even today, you carry this small scar of embarrassment. In fact, this memory has resulted in low self-confidence, especially when you even think of speaking to a group. You recognize that this fear has limited you from achieving greater responsibilities at your job.

Remember the five phases of life (Chapter 1) and how so many moments with long-term impact occurred during the short, early periods of your life? If you shared this story of your embarrassment with colleagues, they might look at you with dismay, and dismiss it as a minor episode of youth. But to you, this incident has become a speed bump in your life. Now is the time to *stop* allowing one high school nightmare to hold you back. After all, you have proved your worth as an adult, that you can succeed in the working world. Additionally, no one at work has a clue as to how much this is a barrier in your life. So, why not make the decision to take the necessary steps to address this problem? Of course, you may not want to make your first speaking engagement the keynote address to a group of 5,000,

but by taking the baby steps first, you might well end up doing that very thing.

Let's return to the garden. Suppose you could use your love of gardening to develop more interests outside of work? For example, you could become the resident expert on roses and the local gardening club might ask you to share your knowledge at their next meeting. By telling your new friends about your passion for roses, you also gain a low-risk opportunity to practice your public-speaking skills on a topic you can be comfortable with. Building a new Brand YOU can be this easy, once you know where you want to go. Take small steps when it comes to big changes, and build self-confidence along the way. As retailing magnate John Wanamaker said, "One may walk over the highest mountain one step at a time."

Starting to Pull It All Together

Based on your Chapter 1 brand audit findings, you will have discovered patterns and learned lessons that can be the basis for change. The Chapter 2 brand image work will fortify your understanding of yourself by showing you how others regard you. Your Chapter 3 brand identity results have helped you realize the great equities you have at your disposal. Especially, by unleashing the passions that surfaced during the brand essence work in Chapter 3, you have a motivating force behind you to enter this proactive step of brand positioning. Remember, however, that brand positioning is meant to bring out the *best* in you, not to set in motion a promotional campaign based on a false image. Continue to be true to yourself, but recognize the power of positioning your brand in a new space of personal fulfillment.

> *"Success is not the key to happiness.*
> *Happiness is the key to success. If you love*
> *what you are doing, you will be successful."*
> —ALBERT SCHWEITZER

Just as with company brands, if you don't craft and implement your positioning plan, others will position you in a way that is convenient for them, based on their first impression of you and their own needs to define you. So, position yourself in a favorable manner; don't allow yourself to be positioned by the competition or others, especially unfavorably. Effective positioning results in a differentiated brand that is competitively advantaged.

Stand for Something!

Brand leaders are always positioned in a relevant space, and are always focused, sacrificing some customers in the bargain to maintain a recognized image. For example, the following well-positioned brands are easy to partner with what each one stands for with its customers.

Brand Name	*What the Brand Stands For*
• Volvo	• Safety
• BMW	• Reliable performance
• Coca-Cola	• Authenticity of taste
• Disney	• Family entertainment
• Michelin	• Safety

- Nordstrom
- Wheaties
- Maytag
- FedEx

- Individual customer service
- Solid nutrition
- Dependability
- Absolutely, positively

Any time a brand identity is either unclear or waivers from its positioning, the product runs the risk of becoming irrelevant in the marketplace—or misunderstood to the point where it sends unintended messages. Consistency of message ensures that the brand avoids confusion and grows its position in the marketplace. This is true for you, too.

YOUR BRAND PERSONALITY

Brand personality is the set of traits that characterize a brand and bring it to life. This personification of a manufactured item or a service is similar to the personalities of celebrities or other public figures who have a certain way about themselves that makes them seem special. Just as corporate and product brands are given human attributes, personal brands are extended by traits that can be clearly defined in other people's minds (i.e., honesty, integrity, compassion, vision, kindness). A car can be called "reliable," "trustworthy," "beautiful," and "fun"; so can people.

Just like a person, a brand has a persona that can come to life in its advertising, packaging, pricing, promotions, and even merchandising. Some brands communicate a personality that is serious, intelligent, or exclusive. Other brands are more approachable, playful, or friendly. There are brands that portray nostalgia, the good times, or authenticity, while others are rendered trendy, cutting

edge, or risk taking. Well—guess what—personalities are part of the brand positioning effort.

Remember also that, when you buy one of these brands, you are also buying into a personality with an image that is manifested in your own brand identity. As we said in Chapter 3, successful brands are best positioned by their focus and their sacrifice. You, as a personal brand, must also focus and sacrifice if your new Brand YOU is to succeed.

Brand personality is the set of traits that characterize a brand and bring it to life.

What is to be your new Brand YOU personality? To get a feel for what kind of thinking you need to do, pick up a copy of *Vanity Fair* magazine and scan the advertisements for hundreds of brands trying to convince you to make a purchase. The women's luxury fashion and fragrance industry is a huge, super-competitive business. Today's winners can be supplanted quickly by tomorrow's new players, so brand positioning is critical for lengthy success. The difference between triumph and failure may well lie in acceptance of a brand's personality by its selected consumers, as well as its ability to translate that personality into store sales. A positioning miss can doom an otherwise high-quality product.

How are these brands presented? What messages are being sent? Did the advertisement peak your interest or turn you away? If you found the tagline offensive, realize that you are likely not the target audience—that manufacturer is willing to sacrifice you

as a prospective customer in order to capture the person who found the ad appealing. See if you are able to distinguish the subtle variations in brand personalities. How does each company set itself apart from the competitors?

More specifically, how would you describe the brand personality for each of the following?

- David Yurman
- Gucci
- Prada
- Dior
- Burberry
- Dolce & Gabbana
- Movado
- Bulgari
- Chanel
- Mikimoto
- Cartier
- Versace
- Tiffany
- DeBeers

What images come to mind with each of these brand names? Do you conjure up pictures of people who might be wearing or using these luxury items? After all, the functional attributes are merely clothes, handbags, perfume, and jewelry. Does anyone actually need a $3,000 purse or a $5,000 outfit—or even higher priced accoutrements? Of course not. So what is the motivating factor for purchase? Well, it varies by shopper, but certainly there is an aspect of the brand identity people are trying to create for their own lives.

There are many ways to attract the attention of prospective customers, even in a super-competitive market segment. In fact, this is where corporate marketers rack their brains to find ways that reach the minds and hearts of their target consumers. What sets these brands apart in such a tight market is brand personality.

BRAND INSISTENCE AND BRAND LOYALTY

There is a step-by-step path (shown in Figure 4.2) that consumers follow in embracing or dismissing a brand, and the top of that path is a hard-won prize commonly called *brand insistence*.

Figure 4.2. The stepping stones to brand insistence.

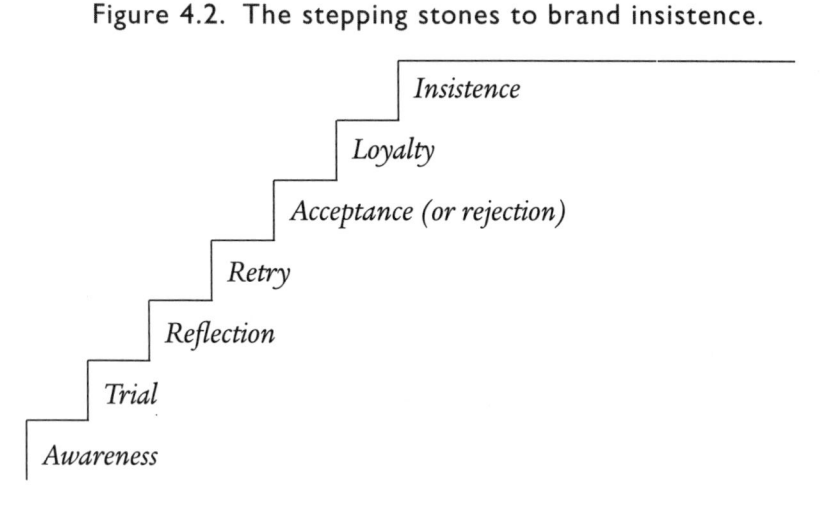

Companies all vie for the loyalty of their target consumers, but earning that loyalty is not easy. Similarly, we all compete in tight markets for recognition, responsibility, admiration, loyalty,

and acceptance in our lives; we all are seeking brand insistence from others.

But how is brand insistence earned? Customers learn about brands in many different ways, whether by word of mouth, from advertising in the media, or during observation. In these encounters, they initiate a mental decision tree for review, evaluation, and consideration. First, they become aware of the brand. This is simply cognition that the brand exists; many brands are never found and become extinct owing to lack of awareness. So, calling attention to a brand is really job-one for any marketer.

Once shoppers find the brand, they determine whether to give it a try. Trial is the first time a consumer experiences a product or service. For instance, you probably recall being offered a free sample in your supermarket, as professional samplers hand out bites of, say, a new preparation of chicken using a special sauce. The company hopes that by providing a "risk-free" sample, you will try—and possibly like—its product. You reflect upon the sample and determine if you have interest in adding it to your shopping cart. If so, you take it home and use the product. If it delivers on its promise, you're likely to repurchase the item. If it doesn't deliver, or if it's just not special enough, you might never buy it again.

People in your world go through a similar process as it relates to your personal brand. Once others (i.e., employers, colleagues, family members, friends, neighbors) are aware of you, they are likely to get closer to you and enter a trial acquaintance. A colleague might ask you for assistance, an employer might assign you a difficult task, a neighbor might request a favor—these are crossroad instances where your personal brand is evaluated. The way you produce and perform defines how your brand is perceived, regarded, trusted, and respected. If you come through positively, just like a product delivering on its promise, your brand will be well re-

garded. If you don't come through well, it's likely your brand will be challenged and people might never call on you again.

Should you exceed expectations, your personal brand will be highly respected, and you will move to brand loyalty, whereby others will prefer your service for the work, the assignment, the responsibility, the favor because they have learned to trust you. Achieving brand loyalty is a very admirable level of acceptance, yet there is one level even more desirable: brand insistence.

The definitive brand position—the platinum-level goal of all brands—is brand insistence. This means that there is no substitute and that nothing else will do. In fact, not only are consumers completely loyal to this brand, but they also will become ambassadors among their friends and colleagues. When that customer continues to *not* buy from any other competitor because you provide more service, more added value, that's brand insistence. For instance, how many times has a consumer driven an extra block, or even a few miles, to find a drive-through Starbucks? How many times has a traveler walked past car rental counter after rental counter to find a preferred company? Restaurant guests request their preferred wine; shoppers scour the drug store for their preferred shampoo. This level of loyalty is no accident. It comes as a result of experiences that perhaps began with a brief initial contact, then repeated positive experiences.

We, as personal brands, must also aspire to this platinum level in our dealings with others. If you build your new Brand YOU so that you are the primary choice of those around you, that they insist on you for the assignment or the friendship, and are loyal to you for the opportunity, you've reached the platinum status. You are recognized as delivering and exceeding others' expectations, your personal brand is highly respected, and you are in the zone of brand insistence.

Brand Insistence, Not Brand Rejection

You see a sign that a new deli sandwich shop has opened and you decide to check it out. Your discovery of this new deli is the first step on the stepping-stone path to brand insistence. So, you step into the deli with high expectations of a freshly made lunch. This is now your trial period for this brand. Unfortunately, there is a 15-minute wait, the shop service is disorderly, and the submarine sandwich isn't all that good. You have just had a negative experience, and it will be difficult for this shop to lure you back. Yet, two weeks later you say to yourself, "What the heck, I'll give this place another chance. After all, it was the grand opening and they were probably just having opening problems." This second time you get service and quality similar to your initial visit. You shake your head and mark this sandwich shop off your list.

Regardless of the many coupons you have received or the shop's convenient location, you are now a *brand rejecter*, and unless you see a sign that says "Under New Management," you are no longer a prospective patron. Also, you are prone to warn your friends about this bad experience. Remember, it's possible to either polish a brand or tarnish it. This deli brand, in your mind, is tarnished. Whereas you could have been a brand ambassador for the operation, you're now a critic.

Don't we all go through the same process with people? How many times can someone be late for an appointment, or unprepared for a meeting, or sloppy in his or her presentation, or demonstrate poor workmanship before we write the brand off, warn our friends or colleagues, and take that person's name off our list? That's why we need to constantly work toward the highest level of personal brand satisfaction. We all hope our personal

brands will be preferred, even insisted upon, by those around us. But how often does that happen?

The brand insistence model is a great way to think about your personal brand. Each time you meet someone new or come in contact with a colleague at work, you are being reviewed, discovered, evaluated, and scrutinized. Do you give people reasons to insist that you are the best person for a project? Or, have you provided bad test moments like the sandwich shop example? Brand insistence takes us back to the formula introduced in the Introduction to this book. It is the consequence of the brand relationship:

$$\text{Promise + experience = relationship}$$

Opportunities for Developing Brand Insistence

There are many opportunities each day to make either a favorable or an unfavorable impression, and these opportunities contribute or detract from your potential new Brand YOU's ability to reach brand insistence. How well do you seize these moments? Are you even aware that these situations are brand trials? Building brand insistence requires you understand what you expect of yourself and what others expect of you. Consistently meeting, or exceeding, expectations will attract loyal followers and insistent customers.

Develop a plan of attack for brand insistence. Think about all the people you encounter each day and how well you come across to them. Judging from the results you've had so far, when people test Brand YOU, do they have a positive enough experience to retry? If not, you have a first-impression gap that limits establishing your brand identity. If you do get a retry, do you receive further acceptance or are you then rejected? If rejected, then you've got work to do.

Consider the example of Neil, a young West Coast sales representative for a giant consumer goods company. Neil's been on the job less than three months. After receiving an irate voicemail message from a customer with a problem concerning a product, Neil called the customer back within 15 minutes. Her response was to tell him, "Thanks for the call back. Do you know I've been doing business with your company for fifteen years and have never received a call back quicker than two, maybe three, days? I really appreciate your call. What's your name again?" Wow! Neil is well on his way to building a positive personal brand, provided he continues to follow up as promptly and professionally as he did with this first complaint call.

Would it surprise you that this customer now wants this rep to handle all her business? Of course not. Neil's trial was successful, and his brand insistence has kicked in. And if Neil leaves this company and goes to a competitor, it's quite possible the customer will follow him and buy his new line because she has become brand loyal.

Remember, brand insistence and brand loyalty don't happen by accident. They are the result of positive action (i.e., Promise + experience = relationship). Similar acceptance of Brand YOU by other people can be as simple as being seen as a positive-minded person. Or, it can mean sending a brief thank-you note to someone who took the time to call you when you were ill. Keep in mind that everything you do or say communicates your Brand YOU and both small and large things matter. When others are brand loyal, they are steadfast in their support and dedication to you.

People's sense of your reliability and trustworthiness is developed over time and grants you credibility; in turn, this credibility results in Brand YOU loyalty. And as your brand image strengthens, this loyalty can become brand insistence. People are now adamant

about your image and you are known for the strength of your character and your positive values. Your brand personality is aligned with your brand positioning, and this has gained you supporters. Indeed, even when you are not around, your friends hold you in high regard and represent your ideals accurately. They insist that you are worthy of responsibility and worth giving you new opportunities that you can pursue. You achieve brand insistence through the steady delivery on your promises. Consistency is the key.

Figure 4.3 shows how a person's actions can either create or destroy brand insistence. In this example, two people react to an opportunity when it arises, with different results. In spite of a poor trial, Mary achieves brand insistence. Even with a great start, Paul falls down in the end. The example shows that no amount of brand positioning can correct a bad encounter that negates an underlying promise.

Thus, achieving brand insistence begins with having a clear picture of your roles and responsibilities. This is as true in your personal life as it is in your professional career. With a true picture of these roles you will be better able to position your new Brand YOU. And with good positioning, you'll be poised to establish credibility, which leads to brand insistence and brand loyalty.

THE JOB DESCRIPTION

Every job has a job description, no matter what the vocation or profession. Use of a job description is common practice in the business world. A typical job description details what is expected by any candidate who applies for that position. Usually included

(text continues on page 130)

Figure 4.3. A tale of two employees.

	SITUATION	PERSON A (MARY)	PERSON B (PAUL)
AWARENESS	Mary and Paul have been with the same company for several years, but have just now been put on a special project with people they have never worked with before.	An e-mail goes out to all project members. Mary receives it and prints it out, but takes no action.	Paul receives the e-mail, phones the project leader, and leaves a voicemail message that declares he is looking forward to the upcoming meeting.
TRIAL	At the first meeting, the project leader opens with introductions, describes the scope of the work, and asks for everyone's pledge of assistance in one of the areas.	Mary introduces herself and immediately signs up for the finance committee. She pledges her commitment to work.	Paul says hello, assuming that the project leader already knows him from the voicemail he left. Paul awaits assignment and winds up on the Process Management Committee, which does not excite him.
REFLECTION	At the next meeting, the project leader reads the minutes from the first meeting and asks the members who is on track and who is not. Opinions are already being formed on how well the members are handling the work.	Mary misses the next committee meeting owing to a conflict.	Paul misses the next committee meeting owing to a conflict.
RETRY	At the next meeting, the project leader again checks on the progress of each committee and hears reports.	The Finance Committee chairperson reports that Mary missed the first meeting, but she caught up on all the material, delivered the required analysis ahead of schedule, and even added an executive review to consolidate the results.	The Process Management Committee chairperson reports that Paul missed the first meeting and has not yet delivered the time and motion study he was assigned. It is now overdue and could set back this aspect of the project.
ACCEPTANCE or REJECTION	As the project leader reports to Senior Management, she assesses where each committee stands relative to the project.	The Finance Committee is on track, moving toward making the important recommendations. Mary has met and exceeded her obligations on this project.	The Process Management Committee is woefully behind schedule and is jeopardizing the success of the entire project. Paul has not fulfilled his responsibilities and seems bored at the meetings.

LOYAL	The project manager is near the end of the work and must ensure all committees are prepared to present to Senior Management	The Finance Committee's work is complete and has been submitted for first-round approvals. Mary has contributed to this work with her time and analytical leadership.	The project manager takes over leadership of the Process Management Committee and replaces the chairperson.
INSISTENCE	At the end of this important special project, the project leader completes the final report to Senior Management. This report includes recommendations as well as assessments of the work of individual committees and their members. Senior Management is using this event as an opportunity to identify promising employees for advancement. (While this objective was not stated at the onset, everyone selected for the task knew the project was a top priority and deserved full attention.)	The final report reflects sound financial recommendations, credited to the committee chairperson. During the briefing, Mary is singled out as a key reason for the successful proposal. The chairperson admits that at first, with no phone call to voice interest, and then the missed meeting, there was concern about her capabilities. But increasingly the chairperson was impressed with Mary. Based on this work, Mary is now on the short list for a promotion. Congratulations! Mary has achieved brand insistence.	The project leader reports on the Process Management Committee's work herself, since she has replaced the committee's head owing to lack of leadership. While the committee's recommendations were approved, there were many questions that would require further work before the project is fully budgeted. During the briefing session with Senior Management, the project leader described her disappointment in Paul's performance—the strong voicemail message led to high expectations that unfortunately were not met. Paul did not step up and volunteer for a committee he could get excited about, so he wound up doing something he had little interest in, and the result was poor work. Based on this experience, Paul is not being considered for a promotion, and in fact his performance has raised new questions regarding his capabilities in his current job. Regrettably, based on poor performance, Paul has fallen from "neutral with potential" to brand rejection.

in this description are the job title and its levels of authority along with a definition of responsibilities and accountabilities. This narrative details requisite skills to perform the tasks and functions. Annual objectives are developed for the job and the employee agrees to meet those objectives in a way that is consistent with the job description.

So much is between the lines of a job description that there are always gray areas. You might be surprised to find out how many people work to achieve only the minimal expectations of a job rather than attempt to set a new standard of excellence that could amaze themselves and others. By looking at your personal situation through the lens of a job description, you may find you're exercising certain abilities that you were unaware of, or even better, that can become the foundation for building your new Brand YOU positioning plan.

Write Your Own Job Description

What if you don't work for a traditional employer? Or you work out of the home? How does this career document correlate with your life? Well, it still applies to you. Regardless of how and where you spend your days, everyone has a job description that lists his or her inherent responsibilities, whether formal or informal, written or verbal. Even if you are not receiving a paycheck, you nevertheless have roles and accountabilities in your life. Most important, you have a *personal* job description. You may be a college student, or a homemaker; you certainly know that you have a job, with functions and responsibilities. You have deliverables—those things you have to do each day—and you either judge yourself for accomplishing them or you are judged by others. So, recognizing

this concept can be more powerful for your personal brand than you probably could have imagined. By understanding your job description, you can then develop a unique and differentiated positioning plan and positioning statement.

Most job descriptions include basically the same information. The document begins with the actual job title. Next, the job is ranked within a department in order to show where the position fits in the company's scheme of things. It is customary also to detail the responsibilities of the role, at least in a broad sense. Additional information sometimes includes the key areas of responsibility and who or what departments work with the position. Of course, every job description names a set of basic qualifications; for example, a delivery agent who will drive a special type of truck needs to be qualified for the appropriate class of vehicle.

Some Examples of Job Descriptions

Figure 4.4 cites three examples of jobs for which there is either a written or an unwritten job description. You may not have thought that being a student could be defined in a job description. Similarly, a job description for homemaker may seem foreign, yet this is a complex and underappreciated job in any situation. Yet these are also positions with responsibilities, authority, and accountability.

While these are sample job descriptions, which are far from complete, you get the picture. Think of the many roles you might fulfill in life and the jobs you do. At the same time as you might be a sales representative for a pharmaceutical company, you might also be a board member of your church, the trustee of a family member's estate, a Girl Scout leader, a player on a fast-pitch softball team, a

Figure 4.4. Examples of job descriptions.

	COLLEGE FRESHMAN	SALES REPRESENTATIVE	HOMEMAKER
Department	General liberal arts (XYZ University)	Commercial Accounts Department	Residence
Reports to	Teachers	Regional Sales Manager	Self and family
Overall Responsibility	Complete required courses to earn a bachelor's degree.	Sell range of home appliances to home-improvement centers.	Manage all day-to-day activities of the home and family.
Key Areas of Responsibility	Attend classes, do homework, take and pass tests. Live in residence hall.	Set appointments, build customer relationships, present product benefits, fulfill orders.	Manage household finances, maintain home cleanliness and safety standards, do laundry, prepare meals, monitor family harmony, and schedule family activities.
Works with	Other students, study groups, teachers, teacher aides, tutors, residence assistants, roommate.	Store managers, purchasing agents, shipping managers, product managers, inventory managers.	Food store employees, bank clerks, e-mail shops, laundry employees, home service providers, cable, TV repair people, delivery agents, spouse, family.
General Qualifications	High school diploma, grade point average, SAT, study habits, ability to work with others, writing skills.	Selling skills, presentation skills, communication skills, customer management, ability to work with others.	Organizational skills, attention to detail, adaptability, ability to work with others, safety knowledge, general repair skills, food preparation skills, financial management skills, communication skills, nurturing abilities.

mom, a wife, a daughter, a sister, and the president of your home-owners' association. Whew! That's a lot of jobs. But not really—that's life! When you think about all of the responsibilities you have accepted, each comes with a definable job description, written or understood.

Continuing our example, consider that you are retired, with nothing but time on your hands. Well, what a great opportunity to think what your new job can be. For example, shift your hobbies or desires into a responsibility; make your time more structured. This will help you crystallize your new goals and set you on a fresh course of action, which will be exciting, invigorating, and productive.

Given the concept that everyone has responsibilities, what is your primary job description? Yes, you may operate in an environment that is relatively predetermined, but you can still differentiate yourself with a brand repositioning effort. Using your standard job description, you create a unique space that you can own, your new brand image.

THE BRAND POSITIONING PLAN

By incorporating some brand positioning as you build your new Brand YOU, you'll create a unique space that you will have *chosen* to occupy. Indeed, positioning a new Brand YOU is a conscious effort to take control of your life—to establish what you stand for and work toward brand loyalty and ultimately brand insistence. This step will take you from where you are today to where you want to be. The brand positioning plan will help you organize

your assets and equities and will allow you to set the tone for your future actions. The plan culminates in a positioning statement that defines the space in life that excites you.

The brand positioning plan will include the following elements:

➤ Your brand audit
➤ Your current brand image
➤ Your desired brand identity (including brand essence and brand equities)
➤ Your brand personality

With the plan, you will leverage your strengths and deal with your gaps, focus on your passion points, direct your efforts toward your target goals, and influence the important people in your life rather than trying to satisfy everyone. The catalyst of the plan is the positioning statement.

THE POSITIONING STATEMENT

Brand development companies craft a positioning statement to describe the space that they expect the brand to occupy (see Figure 4.5). Embedded in this statement are the focal points of a value proposition. A value proposition represents the specific and unique benefits that the consuming population should expect to receive. Most experts feel that the time and effort it takes to craft an articulate positioning statement is worthwhile. That's because all positioning efforts are driven by this statement.

Writing your positioning statement will force you to put into

words your vision of the revitalized, new Brand YOU. Within the positioning statement will be four key components: (1) the target audience; (2) the frame of reference, which defines the category or field of play; (3) a point of difference that creates the differentiation of your brand; and (4) the support statement that offers proof that your brand is real and valid. The following figure is a graphic representation of the brand positioning statement.

Figure 4.5. The elements of the positioning statement.

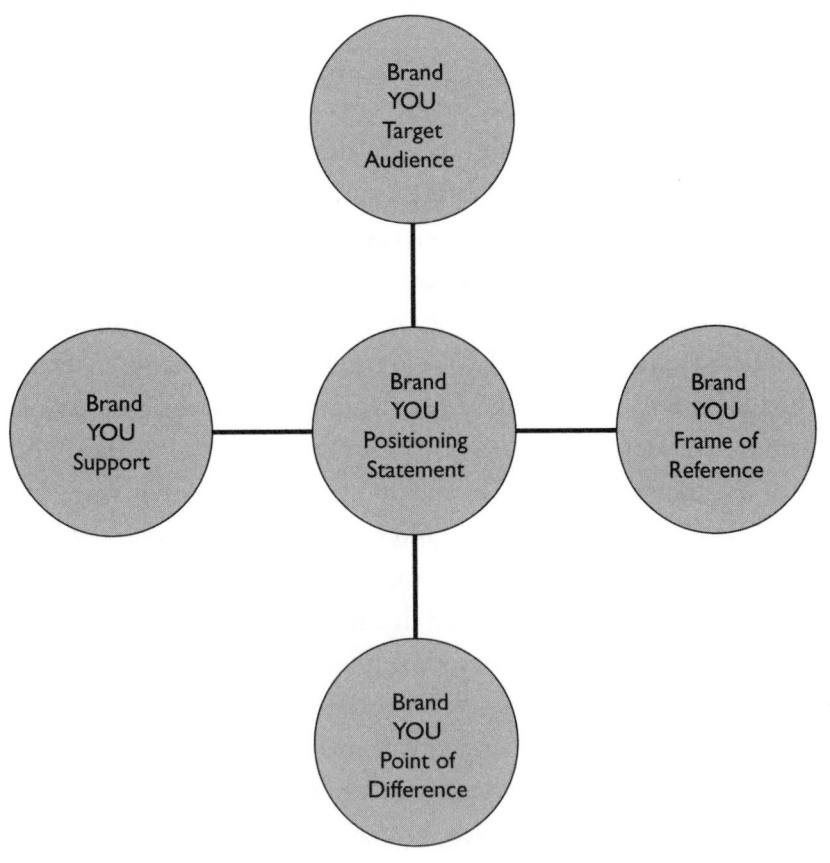

While there are many styles a positioning statement can take, a typical statement follows this general form:

> ➤ To _____ (target audience) _____ .
> ➤ Brand X is _____ (frame of reference) _____ .
> ➤ Who _____ (point of difference) _____ .
> ➤ Because _____ (support) _____ .

Let's take each in turn.

Target Audience

Selecting your *target audience* is the starting point for writing the positioning statement. In corporate branding, the target audience is that group of consumers to whom you are aiming your brand promise, premise, and efforts. If your brand was a rock band, when tickets went on sale, the target audience would be the very first in line to purchase front-row seats. If your brand had a convention to which the public was invited, the target audience would be those people who purchase tickets to attend. The end users are well defined and they are targeted through brand messaging. Note that there are many user groups within any brand's audience; you should not confuse all those users with those you particularly plan to target (remember the sacrifice mentioned in the previous chapter?). Also, as with corporate or product branding, there may well be primary and secondary, even tertiary, targets for your new Brand YOU.

For example, a sporting goods company may choose to target athletes with its repositioning effort, yet want to still attract beginning exercisers. The latter person may have been attracted to the brand because the athletic image was appealing, and the person as-

pires to become an athlete (and hence the brand target). In essence, however, corporate branding teams seek to reach the primary target audience; in the end, the goal is for that target group to become brand insistent.

So, using the example of a brand for a sporting goods company, we fill in the first line of the positioning statement as follows: "To: Women between the ages of 15 and 24, who exercise more than twice a week . . ."

Now, to apply this to personal branding, consider that your target audience is, possibly, a spouse, other family members, friends, community leaders, your employer, your employees, your co-workers, your club members, and colleagues in an industry of your choice. However, your first target audience must always be yourself. If you are not delivering your own brand promise to yourself, then it is impossible to do the same for others. Most people do not think about how they want to see themselves, and this may be the first time you have done so as well. Consider this is an opportunity to get onto paper your vision for your new Brand YOU. Once you have defined who you want to be, you can begin targeting your audiences. Remember, this must not be self-serving; your positioning statement, in essence, describes how the new Brand YOU will be valuable to your target audience. You cannot change others, but you can change how you influence them.

There's one aspect of a personal brand that is different from a consumer brand: you probably will not be able to define your target as a single audience. First, you must meet your personal needs, as mentioned above. So, your important question is, What do I want to stand for, first to myself? In short, what will make you proud of yourself? After all, you are resetting your personal compass to your personal "true north." Have you really been true to yourself, or have you been living someone else's life? Work out a

positioning statement for yourself, then tailor it to your loved ones, your friends, your employer, and so on. Practice with individual statements for each group, and begin with only three or four statements to avoid confusion.

You may ask the question, "How can I be focused while having more than one positioning statement?" First, each statement builds on the same equities you identified earlier. Second, the statements are all consistent with your brand essence. Third, though you will have several statements, you will not be several brands, just one distinct personal brand with different target audiences. There will be only shades of difference among your positioning statements. More than likely, you would like to occupy a different space with your manager at work than with your significant other at home; your statements will reflect that difference. Although you position your brand slightly differently to the Little League team that you coach, to your church elders, to your parents or friends, you will project consistent values and principles to them all. Again, although some consumer brands target several audiences concurrently (i.e., 18- to 24-year-old males who are steak lovers, NASCAR fans who love country music, 7- to 12-year-old children who use PlayStation video games), the consumer brands with more focus always prevail.

Frame of Reference

With corporate branding, *frame of reference* is the point of comparison with other competitors. A brand can compete within a narrow band or extend into a broad array of competitors. Choosing an optimal frame of reference sets the borders within which the brand will compete. For example, Chick-fil-A is a quick-serve restaurant (QSR, or fast food) chain that has distinguished itself with consistent operations, value-based leadership, employee satisfaction, and popular

chicken sandwiches. While this company serves a varied menu, the focus on chicken positions the brand in a distinctive niche that has been successful. This is shown in one of their tag lines, "We didn't invent the chicken. We invented the chicken sandwich."

Chick-fil-A also distinguishes itself in an ongoing campaign of witty commercials and billboard advertisements that show cows urging everyone to "Eat More Chicken" and "Consume More Fowl." The chain's frame of reference is to be an alternative to hamburgers. But the company has another frame of reference: that Sunday is a day of rest, not day of revenue. This is the only major QSR chain in the United States that closes its restaurants on Sunday. This consumer sacrifice has moved the $2 billion, privately owned chain into a position of commitment to employees' welfare (Sundays off) and respect for its faith-based organizational culture. Both tactics produce a discernible, sustainable brand position that sets the brand apart from its competitors.

So, for this example, the frame of reference portion of the positioning statement is as follows: "Chick-fil-A is the anti-hamburger restaurant that observes a day of rest on Sundays."

In the case of personal branding, your frame of reference sets the tone for the space you will occupy. What life category do you want to participate in? Whereas in corporate branding the point of reference is to the competitive set, the frame of reference for your personal brand should be the areas in which you plan to participate and even excel. You establish your brand footprint, so to speak. So, your frame of reference is your field of play, and this field of play is your sphere of your influence, which is more useful in this context than the competitive set.

To continue the comparison, whereas a company's goals for its product brands are to claim an ever-greater percentage of the market by taking share from the competition, this isn't the objective of

your personal brand positioning. The goal of personal brand positioning is to guide you to the position that is optimal for your brand identity. For example, if your job title is that of a salesperson, you may choose your frame of reference to be only other sales representatives in your firm; however, instead you may choose a wider frame of reference, such as all sales reps in your industry. You would simply just have a different field of play. It could also be the local PTA if you want to pursue an elected position, or the corporate task force if you want to be noticed by management, or the industry association award if you want to be considered for that recognition.

Selecting your personal frame of reference helps you establish the topography of your personal brand image. It will also help you envision what success will look like. How high is high? It is fine to set your frame of reference very narrow; after all, you will be implementing the positioning plan as you designed it, so you need to be comfortable with the landscape.

Point of Difference

The *point of difference* is the consumer benefit to the target audience relative to the frame of reference. The benefit should be a unique and recognizable advantage when compared to the competitive offerings. Indeed, the point of difference is the differentiation in the field of play you have chosen for your new Brand YOU.

As with consumer brands, the point of difference for your personal brand will describe the special benefits you provide to your target audiences. For example, an individual who always sends flowers to friends the afternoon before he arrives for dinner establishes a much appreciated point of difference compared to other guests they might invite. Or, the woman who unfailingly sends birthday cards to family, friends, and colleagues establishes a point

of difference, since most people think only of themselves. The youth soccer coach who organizes an annual Halloween game where participants play in costume establishes a point of difference that not everyone may enjoy!

Let's consider an example. One brand that has based its positioning on a real differentiated benefit is the BlackBerry, a wireless handheld device introduced in 1999. Invented by the Canadian firm Research In Motion (RIM), this device took the world by storm when it appeared. With many upgrades and new models, RIM has continued to savor its major point of difference, incorporating Internet connection, photography, and telephone in one device. With the recent entry of the iPhone from Apple, RIM will be challenged to bring further innovation and personal convenience in order to protect its point of difference. Points of difference, especially sustainable and discernible points of difference, are always remembered and are typically inherent in these brands (or products) that succeed. In short, it's better to be remembered than to be recalled. So, with this example, the point of difference is expressed as follows: "With the BlackBerry from RIM, customers can stay connected to the wireless world anywhere, anytime, at home or far away."

What distinctive benefits do you bring to yourself? What distinctive benefits do you bring to important audiences, like your family, co-workers, club members, or colleagues? Whether it be corporate branding, product branding, or personal branding, a sustainable, discernible point of difference, of uniqueness, helps a company, a brand, or a person stand out from the rest.

Support

Support is the evidence that your positioning statement is true, that the point of difference is real. Support for the brand positioning is

vital but it can come in many different forms. For a product brand, support can be evident in market share, strong sales, big profits, large numbers of consumers, high satisfaction scores, and so on. Whatever the measure of confirmation, it should connect directly with the point of difference. Remember, each element in the positioning statement builds on the previous one. Also, it is vital that the support is specific and, if possible, measurable.

To build a strong personal brand positioning statement, you will need credible support. As an example, consider Anna Mary Robertson Moses, "Grandma Moses." She was a lively woman who survived the Great Depression with tenacity and creativity. After years of embroidering, her arthritis made this craft painful and unfulfilling, so she took up painting at the youthful age of 75 years old. Her work was recognized by collectors of American primitive art and was exhibited in fine galleries. Grandma Moses lived to be over 100 years old, and she completed around 1,600 paintings. Obviously, Grandma Moses had support that proves she was a great artist. If she were to write her positioning statement, the support portion would be expressed as follows: "Because: I am a folk artist with an estimated 1,600 paintings to my name, many of which have appeared in the country's finest art galleries."

PULLING THE ELEMENTS TOGETHER

It's time now to shape the brand positioning statement for your new Brand YOU. You can follow this basic form, with only minor modification. The Brand YOU positioning statement will embody the Brand YOU essence that you discovered in Chapter 3. Also, your Brand YOU personality, as also described in Chapter

3, provides the foundation for this positioning statement. The following figure shows just how this is structured.

The template is a logical way to write an articulate statement. You may have written mission statements in the past that define the direction of your company, your product line, your career, or the work of an organization. You also may have written a vision statement to describe where you'd like to be in five years. Though the mission or vision statement may have been clear, for whatever reason you may not have fulfilled that mission or achieved that vision. The difference between those statements and your personal brand positioning statement is that you can be much more pinpointed and direct. So, a personalized brand positioning statement includes the four points discussed above and can easily follow this suggested template:

- To _____ (target audience) _____ .

- I _____ (frame of reference) _____ .

- Who _____ (point of difference) _____ .

- Because _____ (support) _____ .

As an illustration, suppose you are writing a positioning statement as a high school English teacher. Your statement might read something like:

To: *Students who attend my English literature classes*
(target audience)

I: *Am a flash of light that opens the eyes, minds, and hearts of impressionable teenagers*
(frame of reference)

Who: *Motivates young people to see themselves through the classic works of outstanding authors*

(point of difference)

Because: *Class attendance is over 95 percent every day, class partici-pation is contagious, and many students have gone on to major in literature in college or become recognized writers.*

(support)

You can almost feel what it is like to attend this teacher's classes. This is not to suggest that all teachers are *not* like this, but the statement effectively points out what makes this particular teacher special. Can you begin to sense this teacher's brand essence and her accompanying brand personality? Do you recognize the significance of the support at the end? A well-crafted positioning statement should allow the target audience to understand the brand without its being specifically called out or having to be repeated.

It should be our individual objective to have someone quickly know who we are (our personal brand) simply by reading the bullet points of a positioning statement. In corporate and product branding, we call that *aided brand awareness*. Interestingly, by using this template, you can quickly and easily convey who you are, what you stand for, and the space you've decided to occupy. In business, the term "elevator discussion" refers to a three-, four-, or five-sentence descriptor on a company's product. The term originated with the need for businesspeople to quickly (i.e., between floors on an elevator ride) describe their company or product line. Your positioning statement needs to accomplish the same thing.

Think about this positioning statement: "Wal-Mart is a large discount department store that has thousands of products, all providing a wide range of consumers both one-stop shopping and national brands at everyday low prices." It's clear. It's succinct. It can

be said on an elevator between two or three floors And it efficiently defines brand Wal-Mart's positioning.

CORRELATING THE BRAND POSITIONING STATEMENT WITH THE JOB DESCRIPTION

Earlier in this chapter we introduced the concept that everyone has a job description, regardless of whether you receive a paycheck or not, because you have accountability. For the sales representative, the job description in Figure 4.6 outlines what is expected of

Figure 4.6. Sales representative job description.

Job Title:	Sales Representative
Department:	Commercial Accounts Department
Reports to:	Regional Sales Manager
Overview of Role:	Sell a range of home appliances to home improvement centers
Detailed Roles:	Set appointments Build customer relationships Present product benefits Fulfill orders
Works with:	Store managers Purchasing agents Shipping managers Product managers Inventory managers
Qualifications:	Selling skills Presentation skills Communication skills Customer management Ability to work with others

this individual. Now, imagine this person's positioning statement, and you will see how a job description can be expanded or contracted depending on how you think about the role.

Realize that every sales representative has basically the same job description, yet two different employees may view this job with different perspectives. Each wrote a positioning statement to describe the work and time (see Figure 4.7).

Notice how the sales reps attacked their job title (and description) from completely different angles. Sales Representative A chose to follow the job description, focus on his boss as the target audience, and use the performance review as his support. His only point of difference was that he delivers on expectations. Compare him with Sales Representative B and you automatically feel a higher level of intensity. Sales Rep B has identified the target audience as his key customers. His frame of reference is that of being part of their team. The point of difference is that he has become

Figure 4.7. Two variations on a positioning statement.

SALES REPRESENTATIVE A		SALES REPRESENTATIVE B	
To:	My Regional Sales Manager	To:	Executives with my key customers
I:	Meet the requirements of the job,	I:	Am a highly valued extension of their leadership team
Who:	Delivers the expected sales results,	Who:	Proactively brings innovative sales building initiatives to their company,
Because:	My annual performance review says so.	Because:	My company has been named supplier of the year and our sales are up 25% over prior year.

a salesperson who creates value, not just supplying inventory for the customer. And—look at the support—the rep has been named supplier of the year, with double-digit sales growth. Clearly, these are two very different employees. Sales Representative B has created a differentiated position that places him in a different space within his own company.

Now, let's look at three forms of the college graduate's job description and corresponding positioning statements (see Figure 4.8).

Figure 4.8. Three forms of positioning statement for a college graduate.

JOB DESCRIPTION	POSITIONING STATEMENT	
Type 1: Recent college graduate in search of employment.	To:	Brand ME
	I:	Am a confident yet humble college graduate
	Who:	Is prepared to create value for a Fortune 100 company
	Because:	I completed a challenging curriculum, worked part time, and have the work ethic to make a difference from day one.
Type 2: Recent college graduate with gainful employment.	To:	The management of my department
	I:	Am a high-potential long-term player
	Who:	Is an integral member of the team
	Because:	I am accountable, prepared, and timely with my work, while bringing new ideas for growth that have contributed to my department's exceeding its goals last quarter.
Type 3: Recent college graduate in a developing personal relationship.	To:	My significant other
	I:	Am a fun-loving and committed person
	Who:	Is open to developing this relationship further
	Because:	I am truthful, responsible, and sincere while exploring the potential of our relationship's growing over time.

These three examples represent a person who is looking for a job, who found one, and who is in an important relationship with another person. Each statement focuses on who she wants to be with each target audience. The individual statements are built upon the equities of accountability, sincerity, and pride of work. Yet each statement creates unique positioning with the targeted audience. Imagine if you took the time to be so specific with your brand positioning! If you did, you would create a vision of your personal success and a positioning plan that will lead you to your specific objectives.

To summarize, achieving clear brand positioning is critical to the long-term success of any brand, and to do this, the positioning must be unique and differentiated. First, a target audience is identified, a frame of reference is discerned, and a point of difference is identified that is sustainable. Then, you add bona fide support for the position.

By now, the new Brand YOU is taking shape. Stick with the 7 Steps to Creating Your Most Successful Self and you will avoid creating a false positioning that you could never achieve or maintain. Remember, be true to yourself and you will be successful. As Olympic gymnast Mary Lou Retton has said, "Each of us has a fire in our heart for something. It's our goal in life to find it and keep it lit."

JULIE'S POSITIONING STATEMENT

Remember Julie, our young divorcée? She is energized by the possibility of repositioning herself and has tackled this step with full commitment. She began with a chart of what she feels she stands for (see Figure 4.9).

Figure 4.9. Julie's brand identity.

BRAND JULIE	WHAT DOES SHE STAND FOR
Good worker	Reliable
Good with customers	Relationships are important to her
Successful at her home	Independent
Enjoyed being in the high school play	Fun-loving and outgoing
Exited a bad relationship	Willing to make tough decisions and unwilling to tolerate a negative relationship
Wants more in her life	
Close with her mother	Motivated to change
	Trusting

When we last saw Julie, she was beginning to understand that she really does have a lot to offer, but that she is still trying to make everyone happy instead of focusing her efforts on the few people who really matter, starting with herself. Julie had read her job description many times; as the assistant department manager, she used job descriptions with recruits and new employees as well. Still, she hasn't expanded her thinking to deliver more than just the job requirements. She is aware that her job is to:

➤ Manage the cash flow of the department.
➤ Oversee the work of employees in her department.
➤ Help customers make purchasing decisions.
➤ Interact with other departments.
➤ Work with store buyers to obtain consumer feedback on recent inventory.

Julie was interested in this notion of tailoring the positioning statement to different target audiences. Obviously, she would

begin with herself, but after that, who would be her target audience? This question drove her to think about who mattered in her life. She followed the template and crafted three positioning statements.

Positioning Statement 1—Target Audience: Herself

To: Me (Julie).

I: Am a happy, centered, vibrant woman.

Who: Is in complete control of my new life direction.

Because: I have taken my passion for working with people and built a fresh and exciting career that allows me to fulfill my brand essence.

At first, Julie thought this was a bit underwhelming—until she realized that she had become almost a robot in her job description. While she certainly enjoyed the customer interaction and working with her co-workers, this was about the extent of her reward and professional pleasure. It was also clear to her that she was not touching any personal passions and she needed to rethink how best to do this. Still, she was inspired by the thought of gaining more control of her future. Julie chose, as her frame of reference, "happiness, center, and vibrancy"—not her current career. This is a wide field of play for her. Also, Julie chose for her unique point of difference "control."

This step was such an empowering realization for Julie that she is beaming with possibility. Previously she defined her life in terms of her paycheck and now she was facing real inspiration and motivation. Finally, the support for her statement touches upon her

passions and brand essence. Now, Julie has some more work to do in making her positioning statement more specific.

But that was just one of her positioning statements. Remember that Julie identified her mother as another target audience, since she has always relied on her for support. She knows Julie about as well as anyone, and Julie still counts on her. But, Julie has traditionally looked to her mother for specific assistance, bordering on acceptance. Now she wants to reposition this relationship to be more mature.

Positioning Statement 2—Target Audience: Julie's Mother

To: My mother

I: Am a loving and independent daughter with a clear direction in life

Who: Has taken control of her life and found her calling

Because: I am happy, fulfilled, and am treated as a partner when seeking guidance and council rather than approval.

Julie's third target audience was a logical choice, since it was her customers in the department store. At first glance, this does not appear unique or motivational, since this is where she has been for years. However, since this is her current job, why shouldn't she try to reposition herself at work and take it to a higher level? She is skilled and is doing a good job, so this is using her core equity, and it is always a good idea to be well respected at work.

Positioning Statement 3—Target Audience: Julie's Customers

To: My customers, with whom I have developed relationships

I: Am their dedicated personal shopping consultant

Who: Knows how to bring out the very best in each customer

Because: My clients are Brand JULIE insistent, my brand identity is well known throughout the shopping mall as "the best"; I top all others in monthly sales, and all new recruits want to train directly under me.

While Julie was still a little hesitant about her writing ability, she could really feel something inside her moving. She had not had this level of self-confidence anytime in the past. While she was not yet where she wants to be in life, she has quite a bit to be proud of.

Julie really feels good about the three target audiences she has chosen. She thinks that she can handle these three positioning statements and wants to tweak them as she has time. But in general she feels enthusiastic and ready to make some needed changes for the betterment of Brand JULIE.

In conclusion, brand positioning is vital to the success and well-being of any brand, be it a product or a person. Effective brand positioning is a blend of your personal mission, aspirations, and vision. There is no right or wrong positioning; it's a snapshot of where you want to see your new Brand YOU reside.

CHAPTER 5

IF IT'S TO BE, IT'S UP TO ME!

*STEP FIVE: SET YOUR BRAND **YOU** GOALS*

"The will to win means nothing without the will to prepare."
—JUMA IKANGAA, WINNER,
1989 NEW YORK CITY MARATHON

REBRANDING YOURSELF IS A LOT like running a marathon race. You're in it for the long haul, so having clear and simple goals and being well prepared will help you reach the finish without collapsing. You're at Step Five, and it's time to set your branding goals.

You have written your positioning statements, which symbolize the spaces you plan to occupy for each of your target audiences. If you've been true to yourself, these statements reflect who you are deep down inside and who you want to become for the people who matter to you—beginning with yourself. Now you will break

153

down these phrases into specific priorities. To organize your priorities, you need to concentrate on setting your goals. As is said, "In the absence of clearly defined goals, we become strangely loyal to performing daily acts of trivia." Don't let that happen to you!

It is amazing how many people have well-defined objectives for their careers, yet few goals for their personal lives. That situation captures the dramatic difference between earning a living and earning a life. Consider that most businesses have plans that include goals they hope to reach, and sometimes even recognition of the potential barriers to achieving those goals. So why do many people avoid setting goals for the most important business of their lives—their personal and inner beings?

Are you one of these people? Imagine that it is early morning and you have just arisen after a good night's sleep. Without being conscious of it you will set goals for the day. For example, let's say you need to be at work by 8:30 A.M. and the drive is about 25 minutes; you will need to leave no later than 7:50 to allow a cushion for traffic delays. You will mentally select a driving route that is reliable and predictable. Once you arrive at your job, you will likely organize your day to ensure you complete your daily assignments. Then, after lunch, you will begin to think about your evening activities—dinner plans as well as chores and the like. Setting goals is a simple, almost automatic process we all go through every day. Now, think what you would accomplish if you were to formalize your goal-setting to be more thoughtful and more analytical. Oh, the places you could go (and lengths to which you would grow). Setting personal goals is the difference between a vivid dream and reality.

SETTING PERSONAL PRIORITIES

Before launching the process of setting goals, you need to gain a quick overview of how establishing personal priorities can be useful. It is natural to try to solve too many problems or issues at one time; we're rushed to find solutions. But this propensity for impatience reflects too many objectives and diffused efforts. Avoid this trap. To meet your goals, be careful in your choice of objectives and be thoughtful in prioritizing them.

Think of priorities as important areas in your life. In some cases, their importance may be nonnegotiable; in other cases, you may be able to rank them lower. So how do you identify what is and what is not important in your life? Earlier chapters of this book discussed brand focus and sacrifice. These concepts come into play in setting the life priorities that will drive your long- and short-term goals. Sometimes you will find it necessary to forgo immediate gratification so you can achieve a brighter future in the long haul. For instance, a friend may invite you out for a fun evening, yet you know you are committed to attending a lecture that will be beneficial regarding one of your priorities. It is tantalizing to say, "What the heck; let's go out and have a great time together." Yet this distraction will set you back from reaching your goals. The philosopher Albert Camus said, "Life is the sum of all your choices." How you choose to deal with these distractions will be a predictor of your future success.

Your Core Essence

In considering your brand identity, you took time to understand your brand essence—the heart and soul that drive you. This quintessential element of who you are is at the core of your life, even

if you do not feel it active every day. Therefore, as you begin to establish priorities, why not start right there, at the core? After all, priorities of the heart and soul will guide your pursuit of important personal goals.

Reach inside yourself and deliberate your passion points as you set priorities. By asking yourself a few key questions, you can bring to the surface those passions that delight you to your essence. Perhaps, also, this will open your eyes to some gaps in your life. Eliminate your blind spots by shining light on those gaps or weaknesses. For example, the chart in Figure 5.1 groups questions by type. Once you see some patterns in your responses, you can focus on long-term goals.

Time Management

The single most important asset that you manage in your life is time. One quick hour leads to a short day, which leads to a short week, which leads to a short month, and so on. How many times have you been amazed at how tall a neighbor's child has grown in what seemed to be a short time? Or how quickly a building in the neighborhood was built? Or the realization that you haven't seen a friend in months, when you thought it was only weeks? And then you exclaimed, "Time just flies by!"

Think about all the seconds, minutes, hours, days, weeks, and even months that you waste. It's eye-opening. During that time, what did you accomplish? After all, while you weren't looking, a child grew a whole foot taller, a construction team took over an empty lot and constructed a house. The difference is that the building crew had a set of plans and a schedule to follow. What if you had organized your time in a similar way? Imagine how much you could have done to activate your brand positioning. Time

Figure 5.1. Questions for self-examination.

TYPE	QUESTION
Enjoyment	What do you enjoy doing?
Academic	What would you like to learn?
Professional	What do you want to do with your career? How do you want to spend the majority of your waking hours?
Mindset	What do you need to do to live a more positive, productive life?
Creativity	What awakens your imaginative spirit? Is it art, music, theater, reading, traveling?
Well-being	Do you take control over your physical and mental well-being?
Social	Do you have a well-developed network of friends and family? Is that network important to you?
Money	Do you have a long-term financial plan for you and your family? Is it sufficient to realize your goals?
Ecology	How have you given back to your community or environment? Does giving back what you have received matter to you?
Spirituality	Are you at peace with yourself? Do you desire a deeper spiritual connection?
Happiness	What activities make you happy and optimistic about life? How can you spend more time doing these things?
Fulfillment	How do you define *personal fulfillment*?

goes by whether you put it to good use or not. It is a constant of our lives and we are continuously chasing the clock. And you, just like everyone else, too often take time for granted. If you thought of time as a valuable resource, the way we think of money, or gasoline, or electricity, or water, you wouldn't be so carefree with

it. Better managing your time can be a powerful paradigm shift for you.

Time management is a significant aspect of setting effective priorities. In Chapter 3, we explained how a person realistically has only 112 hours of discretionary time each week, after accounting for 8 hours per night resting or sleeping. Managing the available time is already a challenge for most people, and with new priorities, getting everything done becomes even more of a trial. Without saying no to some endeavors, you will not free up enough time to pursue your newfound priorities. What is it about the word *no* that troubles us all and is so hard to say? Yet saying no may well be the key to opening the doors to that new Brand YOU.

Tools for Assessing Priorities

There are two simple exercises for sorting your priorities. These will help you focus on your inner desire to say no, help you avoid wasting time, and encourage you to pursue your dreams. The first task forces you to prioritize your goals. When you grade your current activities, you will see which ones are nice to do and which ones are needed to be done. You may be surprised at how many activities are ancillary to your desires, even though they seem to take precedence at times. Sometimes we focus so much on the nice thing to do because, deep down, we know the need-to-do items take more focus, more time, more energy, and more effort.

So, revisit your average week time balance grid (Figure 3.2), and rank your current activities and responsibilities with a numerical rating. Define them as follows:

1. Positioning critical—super-important, must do
2. Important—need to do

3. Middle of the road—neither important nor unimportant (nice to do)
4. Could do without
5. Positioning unnecessary—why am I doing this?

Then, begin to weed out the "positioning unnecessary" and replace those activities with more valuable ones.

The next exercise asks you the following question and you track the answers on the worksheet in Figure 5.2: What should I stop doing, start doing, and continue doing?

By asking such innocent yet important questions, and categorizing the steps to eliminate unnecessary activities, you will begin to allocate time for those priorities that matter most to you and that will help build the new Brand YOU. Thus, if you look at your current priorities through this lens, you will be forced to reallocate your time. As we mentioned earlier, it is eye-opening to see how you have wasted your time. It is especially enlightening to recognize how much time is spent on middle-of-the-road activities that, in the long run, have little importance for achieving your goals. Time is precious—don't waste it!

Whatever goals you decide to pursue, they will require an inventory of necessary resources and your commitment to apply resources. These resources include time, effort, energy, and money. Any high-priority goal you plan to achieve will involve trade-offs. Some of these decisions will be easier than others, but at the beginning you can at least eliminate the obvious time-wasters that involve serving the needs of others while taking valuable time away from doing more fulfilling things. Setting priorities is always an opportunity for betterment. In our time-constrained world, you have to be proactive when it comes to time management. Things will not change by themselves.

Figure 5.2. Activities change worksheet.

STOP DOING	START DOING	CONTINUE DOING

SETTING GOALS FOR ACHIEVEMENT

Successful businesses, universities, nonprofit organizations, sports teams, rock bands, military operations—any organization or group, for that matter—have one thing in common. They understand the need to focus on top priorities and have established a set of goals, which they plan to achieve. Whether the goal is to win the state football championship, expand their market share in software, capture an enemy camp, or debut as a singer in Carnegie Hall, each sees goal setting as an important step that cannot be taken lightly. Organizations that function without clear goals have perplexed administrators who are confused about what they are expected to deliver. Besides presenting other problems, deficient goal setting leads to wasted time, energy, and talent. And it's impossible to set goals without having clear objectives. Clear objectives are also vital to individuals building a new personal brand.

So, we begin by writing down our goals. The act of committing goals to a sheet of paper forces you to think about what it is you are trying to accomplish. And having your goals down in writing helps avoid misinterpretations and memory lapses. Plus, it serves as a tangible reminder of your goals, worthy of revisiting frequently. At this stage, you need to ask yourself a visionary yet specific question: What does success look like to me? What are my goals?

In 1981, George T. Doran, in an article that appeared in *Management Review*, introduced the concept of SMART goals. SMART is an acronym for Specific, Measurable, Achievable, Relevant, and Time-bound, that is, goals that are *specific* are understandable and simple to communicate to others. Some people tend to complicate matters, especially when it comes to goal setting. It is more difficult to be simple and straightforward than to be complex, but the effort will yield a goal that is specific, not vague and undefined.

Measurable goals have the ability to be checked and tracked. In the case of a business, measurable goals would be profit or sales target levels. In the case of a person, you may want to sell your condominium for $X, and to relocate to a new place by the end of the year. These goals are very measurable. *Achievable* goals are goals that obviously can be achieved or reached. In other words, you have the capability of realizing those goals; they are not "pie in the sky." *Relevant* goals are those that are realistic, that can be met. While you want to set goals that require you to stretch, if they are unreasonable, they are nothing more than pipe dreams. Finally, goals that are *time-bound* are set in a framework of completion—in other words, there's a due date.

A well-written business goal may sound something like this: "By December 31 of this year, Brand X will grow in share of its target market from 23 to 25%, resulting in incremental operating income of $500,000." A well-written personal goal for your new Brand YOU might be: "By December 31 of this year, I will meet with every manager in my division to understand their goals and the skills required to succeed. I will demonstrate my eagerness to create more value for the company and share my experience so that 'I am on their radar screen' for future opportunities."

Well-constructed business goals are meaningful and motivating, and keep us on task. Goal-oriented individuals at work move through the day with a clarity of purpose, which shows up in their daily progress. They understand the reasons behind the goals and how they contribute to the success of the company. Extending the SMART corporate goals to individual employees aligns human resources with common business objectives. This is important because employees often have difficulty linking their specific jobs to the corporate goal. By the same token, applying the SMART ap-

proach to goal-setting to building your new Brand YOU will bring your personal resources into alignment.

Well-constructed goals are meaningful and motivating.

Applying the SMART Goals to Your Personal Brand

Successful brands are the product of specific goals: sales targets, market share, consumer preference, growth, and so on. While your new Brand YOU may not have such measurable goals, nonetheless you need to lay out your own objectives. Then, you will develop the action plan with the when, what, where, how, and who you will reach those objectives.

Successful brands are the product of specific goals.

Having written your brand positioning statements, you have a good picture of what your new Brand YOU looks like. Your personal and professional aspirations will guide you in setting your new goals, and the process begins with reviewing those positioning statements. Since these branding statements are visionary and customized, make sure they reflect the spaces you want to occupy. Since the goals you will set for yourself are designed to accomplish your positioning statements, those statements need to be perfect for your objectives.

Follow the SMART principle, as explained above, keeping the five points—Specific, Measurable, Achievable, Relevant, Time-bound—in mind. Consider:

- ➤ Where do I want to be in 10 years?
- ➤ Where do I want to be in the next 12 to 24 months?
- ➤ What are my concerns, problems, challenges, and anxieties about the goals I have set for myself?
- ➤ What are some likely barriers, both controllable and uncontrollable, that could arise and stand in the way of my achieving my goals?
- ➤ Other than myself, who will I rely on to help me achieve my goals?
- ➤ What major changes in my physical, mental, and spiritual being will I need to make to accomplish my goals?
- ➤ How will I feel when I get to where I want to be?
- ➤ What type of work will I be doing?
- ➤ Will I be in better physical shape?
- ➤ Who will I be spending time with?
- ➤ How will my life have changed?
- ➤ What will be different?
- ➤ What will I have stopped doing?
- ➤ What will I have started doing?
- ➤ How will I monitor my progress and stay on track?
- ➤ Are these goals worth pursuing?
- ➤ Am I passionate enough to follow through?

These broad questions, and other soul-searching inquiries, will help you establish your goals. Rather than be too pinpointed, allow yourself to have a more general view. Set a few broad

goals that create corridors for more detailed action plans in the next steps.

Long-Term Brand YOU Goals

The best place to start building Brand YOU goals is to think long term. While the horizon will vary by person, you may look as far as 10 to 20 years ahead. Other people may find 5 to 10 years more realistic. Regardless of the time line, long-term thinking is an important first phase. What do you want your life to be like in three, or five, or ten years? Where would you like to be living? What would you like to be doing with your time and friends? What will you have done with your life by then? From these larger goals will come the smaller, personal targets.

These long-term goals will start your juices flowing. These are legacy questions. What do you want to be remembered for in your life? Setting long-term goals aligned with your priorities will inspire you to action, change, and transformation. After all, until you take time to dream about the future, you won't be able to imagine a set of goals for your life. Lines from the great Rodgers and Hammerstein musical *South Pacific* say it all: "You gotta have a dream. If you don't have a dream, how you gonna have a dream come true?" Remember, establishing a few powerful long-term goals (less than five) is more pragmatic than having several widely disparate goals. By the way, just because you have identified several high priorities, you need not have independent goals for each. If you see overlap, combine them into a few grand long-term goals.

Flexibility is another key element in setting long-term goals. Things will happen along the way that will necessitate your

changing and modifying those goals. Adaptability in achieving your goals will be an important capability.

Flexibility is a key element in achieving long-term goals.

Short-Term Brand YOU Goals

Your long-term personal goals provide direction for setting your short-term goals. In fact, this is a good opportunity to recognize the difference between short- and long-term personal goals. In effect, short-term goals can be viewed as objectives, while long-term goals are expectations of something higher in magnitude. Think of objectives more as tactical targets that will direct your short-term activities.

For instance, short-term goals are usually between 12 and 24 months in duration. These are the goals that move you closer to the long-term goals. Suppose you determine that in 10 years you want to be recognized as a culinary expert. In fact, you have set a goal that within 10 years you will open your own cooking school to train up-and-coming chefs. Cooking awakens your inner passions, and already you are an avid home cook. You see this field as truly motivating you. However, right now you are working as a flight attendant. And while you are a good cook, you have years of schooling, as well as a lengthy apprenticeship, ahead of you, not to mention being a professional chef for many years before you are in a position to open your own restaurant. No fear, though, because this is a long-term goal and you have several years to get your plan in place.

You will spend your time over the next couple of years advanc-

ing to the realization of that dream. Fortunately, your flight attendant's schedule provides enough time off to enroll in a cooking school and begin to take your home-grown skills to the next level. So, you now have a line of sight on your short-term goal. You may even choose to parlay this training into a networking opportunity to obtain a part-time position in a commercial kitchen. By getting to know restaurant suppliers and owners, you can slowly build your network for contacts you'll use later on. Perhaps you might assist a catering company on weekends, where you can display your cooking, presentation, and client management skills. Plan each step of the way with vision of your goals, and you'll be off and running toward realizing your dream.

You can lay out short-term goals that will contribute to your long-term goals. As the previous example illustrates, people can chase their dreams while gainfully employed elsewhere. You can punch someone else's clock while you start piecing together your new Brand YOU.

This goal-setting exercise is an opportunity to reach for your dreams. There is no reason to exist in an environment that is unhealthy for you or less than fulfilling. Health and fulfillment directly correlate to achieving your goals, big or small. We've all heard people say "I'm living the dream." We can all live the dream, but first we have to formulate that dream. Take this moment to believe in yourself and your abilities.

Remember all of the brand equities you identified in Chapter 3? Do you recall that special brand essence that is inside of you? This is your heart and soul longing to get out. If you have the dream job, that's great, but don't miss a chance to leverage that dream job into your dream personal life. After all, there's a future for those who plan for it—and dream of it.

---

*The goal-setting exercise is an opportunity
to reach for your dreams.*

A Business Example

Wal-Mart is a great example of a brand with a simple and clear goal: to deliver the lowest prices every day. In fact, its mantra is "National brands at everyday low prices." This global brand has a written goal that is transparent to all consumers, and by being consistent, the brand occupies a strong position in the marketplace. Wal-Mart maximizes its supply chain and overhead expenses to allow low prices to prevail. Through its high-volume sales and aggressive price negotiations with suppliers, Wal-Mart is able to achieve its goal.

Imagine, for a moment, that Wal-Mart elected to reposition its goal to be the favorite store for innovative, highly creative, and dynamic décor packages for homes. Or, perhaps it wanted to reposition to become the mass merchandiser known for high-end jewelry or watches. Or perhaps its new goal was to be the store that provides incredibly high levels of customer service, all for higher price points. This would result in an entirely new brand positioning and would have a material impact on Wal-Mart's position in the marketplace. But by remaining steadfast in its goal to achieve and maintain low pricing, Wal-Mart commands the leadership position in its field of value retailers. That's because brands must remain true to themselves, consistent and dedicated to their core principles, their positioning, and their ultimate goals.

Imagine if your new Brand YOU had goals as clearly stated and

as well communicated as does Wal-Mart. If you did, you would be assured of clear Brand YOU communication, and your activities would be well focused on your goals. Your SMART goals, then, are a beacon for measuring your success. Your happiness level can be significantly improved while you endeavor to reach your goals, be they personal or professional.

Brands must remain true to themselves, consistent with and dedicated to their principles, positioning, and goals.

With specific goals, you will be able to transition from the brand you are to the brand you want to become. Measurable goals will ensure that they become more than just words on paper. Your goals need to be realistic but also achievable—be possible to meet while also involving a bit of risk. After all, you shouldn't be asking yourself, "What is the risk I'm taking if I do this?" You should be asking, "What is the risk I'm taking if I *don't* do this?" Not doing something that is to your benefit is usually a greater risk than maintaining the status quo. You need to be brutally honest with yourself about your life—about how great, good, neutral, or bad you feel about your career, your company, your product or service, and your personal life.

As mentioned above, your goals will determine the strategies and actions that you will follow, so think seriously about these for a few days. Come back to this goal-setting exercise several times. Ask the question, Will achieving these goals align with my positioning statements? If not, then rethink your goals. But let's catch up with Julie, to see how she has stated her goals.

JULIE'S GOALS

Julie was last seen setting her priorities and writing her brand positioning statements. She thought setting the goals next would be a cinch with her three positioning statements under her belt, but this task has proved more challenging than she expected. When she completed the time balance grid earlier she found that she was doing a lot of things in her available 112 hours per week that she would like to stop doing. She was also pleased to see she was spending so many hours doing things that she is good at and enjoys. Let's revisit her positioning statements, one at a time, and then go from there.

*Positioning Statement 1 (Herself):

To:	Me (Julie)
I:	Am a happy, centered, vibrant woman
Who:	Is in complete control of my new life direction
Because:	I have taken my passion for working with people and built a fresh and exciting career that allows me to fulfill my brand essence.

*Positioning Statement 2 (Her Mother):

To:	My Mother
I:	Am a loving and independent daughter with a clear direction in life
Who:	Has taken control of her life and really found her calling

Because: I am happy, fulfilled, and is treated as a partner when seeking guidance and counsel rather than approval.

*Positioning Statement 3 (Her Customers):

To: My customers with whom I have developed relationships

I: Am their dedicated personal shopping consultant

Who: Knows how to bring out the very best in each customer

Because: My clients are Brand JULIE insistent, my brand identity is well known throughout the entire shopping mall as "the best"; I top all others in monthly sales, and all new recruits want to train directly under me.

Julie is happy with her positioning statements, so she begins the work of goal setting. She looks at her life as a 28-year-old professional retailer and asks the key questions: Where do I want to be in 10 years? What will I be doing? Julie had never really contemplated such a long-term view of her life. Based on the past 10 years, she quickly realized that, in lieu of any new goals, she would probably be working in the same department store, with the same customers, and living in the same apartment.

As Julie took this 10-year look into her future, she became uneasy and a bit confused. "After all, how can I pretend to look ten years down the line when I can barely pay the bills today?" she asked herself. She considered stopping the 7 Steps to Creating Your Most Successful Self in despair. Then she realized that she had absolutely nothing to lose by dreaming a little. She was committed to a personal transformation, so she continued her fantastic voyage.

Julie knew that she would need to find goals that aligned with her three positioning statements. She highlighted the key words out of each positioning statement and looked for common elements. The chart in Figure 5.3 shows her thinking.

Julie could see a lot of similarities in each positioning statement that applied to where she wanted to be when she is 38 years old. Ten years from now, she hopes to be viewed as a respected business leader who serves other people. This goal is a lofty one because today she is a low-level assistant manager rather than a business leader. While she does get high accolades for training the new hires, she feels this is a far cry from impacting the lives of others. Frankly, Julie is struggling with whether or not this is a SMART goal, but she can begin the work of building her new Brand JULIE, so she goes with it.

Consistent with her positioning statements, Julie also meets with her mother to elevate their relationship to a partnership. Julie explains to her mother about her brand repositioning project. At first, she is a bit shy about sharing this with her mother, but her mother offers nothing but positive reinforcement She

Figure 5.3. Brand JULIE comparison of positioning statements.

POSITIONING STATEMENT I (HERSELF)	POSITIONING STATEMENT 2 (HER MOTHER)	POSITIONING 3 (HER CUSTOMERS)
Happy and centered	Clear direction in life	Personal shopping consultant
In control of my life	In control of my life	Bring out the best in people
Have fresh, exciting career	Found my calling	Brand JULIE insistence
Fulfilling my brand essence	Happy and fulfilled partner	"The Best" in the mall
		Trainer of choice for new recruits

tells Julie that while she is very proud of her accomplishments, she has always thought that her daughter had more potential than her current situation shows. She had not been comfortable enough to share this with Julie before, but now that she is aware of this commitment, her mother provides some helpful advice and thoughts that reinforce her willingness to play the role of a partner and trusted advisor. Based on these comments, Julie finds a new sense of inspiration to achieving her short-term goals. These goals will contribute to all three of her customized positioning statements.

Now, let's look at Julie's short-term goals. Over the next two to five years, Julie has chosen four big goals to pursue.

1. Pursue and achieve a bachelor's degree within five years.
2. Build a personal system for being the top customer relations leader in the mall over the next 12 months.
3. Reenter the theater, in some form, over the next 12 months.
4. Improve personal happiness through a fresh health and wellness program within 90 days.

The thought of returning to school at this age was a bit disconcerting to Julie, especially with the memory of her father's high academic standards and imposed pressure. However, if she is going to advance her career and become a leader in 10 years, as planned, she is determined to give it a go. Julie is also concerned about the incremental tuition cost associated with this decision, but she decides to let the discussion with the admissions counselor serve as the information source she was seeking and not jump to any conclusions, especially negative ones. She thought perhaps there would be some kind of financial assistance that she could qualify for. The

10-year time line gives her the perspective to consider a commitment to college.

The other goals feel very doable, and she is looking forward to building herself into the top retail advisor in the mall. The one goal that surprised her most was her commitment to investigate joining a local theater group. With such a low down-side risk, why not check it out? To this day, she has delightful memories of that high school play. If she is successful in achieving these short-term goals, her success will contribute to her meeting the long-term goals.

As it always does, reality has set in for Julie. She realizes that she can barely make her calendar work today; how in the world will she find time to fit all this new stuff in? So, she takes a hard look at her time balance grid once again. To review this yourself, see Figure 3.5. Julie studied the grid, juggled the time frames, and estimated how much time each of her new short-term goals would take to accomplish. Her conclusions are as follows (see Figure 5.4):

Julie was surprised by the thought of 22 additional hours per week, but even more so with the 34-hour realization once she began her college work. For now, she thought, "This is not going to distract me from my goals. These are life-changing goals, and I

Figure 5.4 Brand JULIE new time demands.

	HOURS/WEEK AT FIRST	**HOURS/WEEK IN 6 MONTHS**
Goal 1 (School)	6	20+
Goal 2 (Database)	10	3
Goal 3 (Theater)	2	5
Goal 4 (Fitness)	4	6
TOTAL	22	34

have come way too far to turn back now." However, Julie realized something must give way, so she made some hard decisions to free up time. She began with those activities she could stop doing and not miss. Obviously, there are many things that she is doing that need to be continued, but Julie believes she may be able to better use some of the existing time. She made up a new chart, as follows (see Figure 5.5):

Figure 5.5. Brand JULIE better use of time.

STOP DOING	START DOING	CONTINUE DOING
• 2 hours of weekend coffee with friends. Use for data entry. • 10 hours of grab-and-go meals. Use weekend shopping to better plan for the upcoming week and eat at home. This saves time and money. • Cut 3 hours out of the commute by traveling during off hours to get to the YMCA early, work out, and then go to work.	• Join the local YMCA (good price, equipment, free training advice, and new people to meet). Add 1 more hour of exercise to get to the 4 hours per week of fitness work. • Add 3 hours for home cooking for incremental meals. • Add 2 hours for database management of customer information. • Add 6 hours of college prep work, SAT study, application, advisor meetings, etc. • Add 2 hours for weekend theater activities.	• 3 hours of exercise, but shift to the YMCA program with better results. • 25 hours of customer service, but add a standard profile collection questioning for top 25 clients to build database. • 3 hours worth of mother as partner discussions. • 2 hours of reading. • 10 hours of cooking. • 3 hours of laundry. • 7 hours of commute time. • 15 hours of other work requirements.
• 15 hours found.	• 14 hours added back.	• 68 hours of work and obligations.

Julie was surprised at the relative ease with which she could juggle her schedule. In fact, she went from 83 hours per week of activities to 82 hours, and she has replaced several unrewarding time-eaters with new interests. Yes, this plan will require some modifications in her life—like getting up earlier to get to the gym—but even this is exciting, inasmuch as it is an opportunity to meet new people. She is able to take advantage of a new-member program so the monthly fee is less than the cost of the meals she has been eating out. She had been thinking about getting out of her weekend coffee obligation with friends because it had become more of a weekly gripe session. Eliminating that actually gave her newfound energy and a positive feeling about her future.

She is also amazed at how well her time is being managed and is proud of herself for taking control. Although a bit nervous about both the time and the focus required to succeed in her college education, she has given herself a few months to figure out a system and get psyched for the opportunity. All in all, Julie is beginning to take ownership of her life and focus on her goals. Sure, she has made some trade-offs, but the new activities, new things to learn, new time management, and greater exercise, her prospects for obtaining both a college education and a return to the theater puts Julie well on her way to becoming a brand new Brand JULIE.

CHAPTER 6

I CAN BUILD MY OWN PERSONAL ROADMAP ON MY OWN TERMS

*STEP 6: ESTABLISH YOUR BRAND **YOU** STRATEGIES*

> "Success is no exclusive club. It is open to each individual who has the courage to choose his own goal and go after it. It is from this forward motion that human growth springs, and out of it comes the human essence known as character."
> —HOWARD WHITMAN

THE WORD *STRATEGY* IS overused and misused; it crops up in so many situations to describe so many kinds of actions that it has lost all meaning. Executive after executive has pushed aside papers, presentations, and plans prepared by employees, claiming they were not "strategic" or were too "tactical," or that the presenters were confusing *strategy* with *objectives*. What exactly is a strategy? Suf-

fer no more confusion. For our purposes, *strategy* is simply the answers to the following questions:

> ➤ How do you accomplish your goals?
> ➤ What options are available to achieve your objectives?
> ➤ How do you eliminate any barriers to achieving your goals?
> ➤ How do you leverage your strengths to achieve your new positioning and aspirations?
> ➤ What are your choices to attain your desired positioning?
> ➤ How do you turn dreams into reality?
> ➤ How do you achieve our targeted results?

The late Peter Drucker, management guru, defined *strategy* as "the science and art of using all the forces available to you to effectively execute your plan and accomplish your well thought out goals." That is, strategy is the science and art of using all the forces available to you to execute your plan and accomplish your goals.

Perhaps an example is the best way to define the term. Let's say that a friend asks you to develop a strategy for getting him from Washington, D.C., to Los Angeles, California. On the surface, this seems simple. Your answer might be found by searching online for flight schedules and airline deals. Once you've found your friend a great airfare and some good alternative flights, you then suggest that he take a cab to Reagan National Airport, then catch the flight to LAX and have him pay for the ticket with his credit card. After all, this strategy will accomplish what your friend has requested—or will it?

With no discussion of your friend's goal, your suggestion is merely a good guess. To truly provide your friend with a workable strategy, you need to know a bit more about his objectives—then

you would be in a better position to recommend the optimal strategy. For instance, what if your friend wanted to fly only an American airline? What if he was interested only in flying first class? Suppose he was staying closer to Dulles International Airport? What if he could only make the last flight out in the evening? And the what-if questions go on, making a very important point here. Strategy is developed only after specific objectives and goals have been defined. Strategy also takes into consideration available resources (i.e., what if your friend had only $500 to spend on his trip?) and realistic aspirations.

Now, let's reconsider this recommendation. You try to better understand his goal and receive this picture of success:

"Well," your friend responds, "I have always wanted to see America, and I thought a cross-country tour from our nation's capital to southern California would be just the ticket. You see, time is really no object, as I have a month to make the journey. My car is in tip-top shape, and I am looking forward to seeing some of the great sights of our country. I would like to stay in some small bed-and-breakfast inns along the way as well. I also want to combine big-city tours with visits to a few national parks. This is a trip I have dreamed of for many years, so I want a clear itinerary yet be nimble enough to take in special opportunities along the way. As long as I am back here within 30 days, I am pretty much open to any ideas you have for me to enjoy this great country. And so, my good friend, what is your suggested strategy for me to accomplish this?"

Obviously, an airplane trip will not accomplish this goal. You realize that your friend has multiple options for accomplishing his vision of this "American Dream Vacation Tour." You now begin to uncover some potential barriers to this clear goal. First, there are so many places to visit that it is almost impossible to know which are the best for your friend.

Next, while your friend has 30 days to make the trip, it is in the dead of winter, so travel by car can be an unpredictable mode of transportation unless the route is southernmost. Unfortunately, your friend must travel in winter or the time off from work will disappear. While he is in good physical shape, the thought of a solo road trip makes you feel uncomfortable. What if something happens along the way? Wouldn't a companion be a good idea for safety and enjoyment's sake?

Finally, while the car is in tiptop shape, it also has 100,000 miles on the odometer, which risks engine failure on such a long trip. On the strength side, though, your friend is flexible so you could devise a southern travel route that avoids the worst weather. The safety concern can be minimized with a national-coverage mobile phone, AAA membership, daily e-mail for trip updates, and use of major roads. So, you see, there are many important questions to answer before landing on the best strategy for this trip of a lifetime.

Similarly, strategic planning is an important step in your journey toward a new Brand YOU. Gathering the details for your friend's trip is similar to the dialogue you need to have with yourself before you devise the strategy for achieving your new self. Once you know what success looks like, you can strategically figure out how to make it happen. The "how to make it happen" is your strategy.

AN OVERVIEW OF THE STRATEGIC PLANNING PROCESS

Goal-setting was discussed in Chapter 5. With that step you made an important commitment toward building your new personal brand. You set expectations for yourself and selected a

way to check your progress. Accomplishing your SMART goals depends on your ability to choose the best strategic options, eliminate personal barriers, and maximize individual strengths. You are now at Step 6 of the 7 Steps to Creating Your Most Successful Self. Remember, though, that effective strategies will rely on well-defined goals. You will now use those short- and long-term goals to build action-packed strategies. Bear in mind that there are many potential paths to your destination. Now is the time to assess those options and make the strategic choices to best achieve your goals. Whether you call it surveillance, due diligence, situation analysis, or even market intelligence, you must analyze all the known (and anticipated) variables, obstacles, and challenges you might face in your quest. And you will want to understand each of your options before locking in one strategic plan.

Learning from Brand Strategies

The brand strategies formed during the corporate strategic planning process can be models for shaping your personal brand strategy. Businesses that are committed to building strong brands follow a particular process when it comes to strategic planning. They ensure that the consumer remains at the forefront, while building shareowner value through sustainable economic growth. This process varies from company to company, but all are similar in certain ways. For example, the process is designed to raise key questions, and these questions have parallels with the personal brand-building model.

> ➤ Do the company's leaders believe that greater market share can be achieved through internal brand growth or is it

better to acquire an emerging product that can bring value more quickly?

> Should the company focus on core products in new markets or pursue aggressive research and development to introduce new brands for existing markets?

> What strategic options will lead to the biggest opportunities?

> Does the cost justify the benefit?

> What capabilities are required to meet changing customer needs?

These and many other important questions can be answered easily when all the relevant options are on the table for review. Strategic choices are made after time is spent looking at possibilities. At the end of the day, no strategy is risk free, so businesses must go with their best bet on what will be the most successful path. In the case of Brand YOU, consider that there are alternative strategic choices as well. Let's say, for instance, your goal is to become elected to your community's school board. For discussion's sake, let's also define your key positioning strategies as (1) alliance and alignment, (2) differentiation, (3) education and inspiration, and (4) activism.

In terms of alliance and alignment, you believe that aligning with powerful community leaders and highly respected educators will position you as a colleague of the "movers and shakers." Your strategy for differentiation would position you as a candidate who always seems to take the road not taken. In other words, if all your competitors are knocking on doors visiting community members while wearing a jacket and tie, you knock on doors in a running suit. To support your strategy of education and inspiration, you hold workshops to demonstrate your knowledge of the subject,

your ideas for improvement, and to educate the voting populace. Finally, your strategy of activism would have you participating at every town hall meeting, every community open forum, and every rally. You would join as many organizations as possible to demonstrate your dedication to the community.

These four strategies would help you build that new Brand YOU by conveying your energy, savvy, community spirit, uniqueness, and willingness to serve. In going back to Peter Drucker's definition of *strategy*, you would be using all the forces available to you to effectively execute your goal of winning the school board election. Let's review: You had well-defined goals. You thoughtfully developed four strategies, and you established your brand identity to your potential audience. Seems like a pretty successful campaign, doesn't it? Obviously, the proof is in the election, but your effort follows the process.

Categorizing Your Opportunities

Goals without bona fide support plans, or strategies, are hollow statements. That is why organizations go to great lengths to draw detailed roadmaps during their strategic planning process. Roadmaps provide a comprehensive view of the landscape for any business. They are based on the company's mission statement, its corporate culture, and its strengths and weaknesses as well as its opportunities and threats. The strategic planning occurs at the corporate, strategic-business, and operating-unit levels to ensure alignment throughout the organization. The payoff is a decision to allocate people, time, and money to the highest priority activities.

This same process applies to individuals developing their personal brands. Although the magnitude of resource allocation and

focus on shareholder value don't exist in the Brand YOU process, all the other areas surely do. So, when setting your strategy, ask three key questions:

1. What strategic options are available and should be considered?
2. What are the barriers to capturing these high-leverage opportunities?
3. What strengths do I possess to activate the strategy?

The answers to these questions will drive your strategies to eliminate barriers or pick up the pace to maximize your opportunities. Using the school board election example, and considering Question 1, you could have focused on all four stated strategies or just one of the options. Question 2 could be answered that you had few contacts to help you initiate your campaign, or perhaps those you targeted for alliance had associations with other candidates. Question 3 could be answered that perhaps your greatest strength is your public speaking ability. That would help you in conducting the workshops. Finally, the roadmap details the activities that must be implemented so as to achieve the strategies. The chart in Figure 6.1 illustrates this process for a product brand. This approach is referred to as an *opportunity-based strategic planning process* and it allows a company to view its business from a growth-potential perspective rather than a historical year-end-plus view.

By illuminating the areas of potential brand growth, the roadmap leads to a discussion of how much opportunity the company can capture in the planned period. This becomes a healthy dialogue, enlightening to the people who must eventually implement

Figure 6.1. Opportunity-based strategic planning process for a product.

TOTAL OPPORTUNITY ASSESSMENT	HIGH-LEVERAGE OPPORTUNITIES	BARRIERS TO CAPTURING HIGH-LEVERAGE OPPORTUNITIES	STRATEGIES TO ELIMINATE THE BARRIERS TO THE HIGH-LEVERAGE OPPORTUNITIES	EXECUTION PLANS TO IMPLEMENT THE STRATEGIES
Unfiltered view of the opportunities. Traditional paradigms cannot hold back fresh thinking. Even if the opportunity seems unattainable, now is the time to consider this idea.	Opportunities that seem realistic to achieve. Pursuit based on competitive set, value creation, cost-benefit analysis, etc.	Material realities that currently exist and if left unattended will minimize your chance of achieving your goals.	Elimination of barriers while fulfilling regulations and maintaining internal code of conduct.	Action plans to achieve the strategies.

the business plans. It traditionally creates a different way of thinking within a company and generally shows how much opportunity an organization can consider pursuing. Similar to the way it is helpful in corporate strategic planning, this type of open thinking can be of benefit to your strategic planning for the new Brand YOU. You have decided where you want to go; the question now shifts to how to get there. That's the strategy part. If you take it for granted that you will automatically reach your goals, you will be disappointed. In fact, the hard work is just about to begin. Fortunately, you have completed the reflective work and have on paper your brand positioning statements as motivation.

THE STRATEGIC PLANNING MODEL FOR YOUR PERSONAL BRAND

Your personal brand has many more strategic options than you may recognize on the surface. A slight modification of the corporate approach described above results in a Brand YOU opportunity-based strategic planning model, which pinpoints your many options. Given that you have already tested the waters with your Brand YOU audit, your Brand YOU image, your Brand YOU identity, your Brand YOU positioning statements, and your Brand YOU short- and long-term goals, you are well on your way to devising your strategic plan.

Begin with your positioning statements, transferring them to the first column of the worksheet in Figure 6.2. Then fill in your long-term and short-term goals, using shortened or abbreviated versions to fit the space. Follow that by filling in the column of potential barriers, then list your possible strategic options. You'll have to brainstorm those options, writing down everything that comes to mind. Then whittle the list down to the few that will have the biggest impact. If this seems difficult to determine, consider each strategy option in terms of its pros and cons. What are the benefits? What are the downsides?

Figure 6.2 provides a worksheet for you to use in assessing your own strategic options. Whereas we showed you the implementation stage of the strategic process for the brand, at this point you are developing the strategy associated with your Brand YOU positioning statements. The action plan, or implementation, will be your final step in the 7 Steps to Creating Your Most Successful Self.

Figure 6.2. Brand YOU strategic planning worksheet.

POSITIONING STATEMENTS	LONG-TERM GOALS	SHORT-TERM GOALS	BARRIERS TO ACHIEVING GOALS	STRATEGIC OPTIONS

"Starving Actor" Example

Filling in this worksheet is not all that complicated, but the best way to explain this step is to share an example involving a fictitious "starving actor," which you will find in Figure 6.3.

This young actor is 24 years old and is supporting himself as a waiter but dreams about getting "discovered." He has followed the steps in our process and reached the strategic planning stage, as shown.

As this "starving actor" example indicates, he has come up with various strategic options that merit serious consideration. If, after 10 years of pursuing his goal, the actor has landed the big role, he will have achieved it by leveraging his equities and sticking to his goals. If he does not land that role, he will be 34 years old, and in the process will have developed a wide network of contacts who can help him in a repositioning effort.

SELECTING THE VIABLE STRATEGIC OPTIONS

After listing all possible strategic options, you will need to narrow these down to a few prime choices. Otherwise, you will be putting only a little effort into a lot of initiatives, which will yield small results. Remember, in strategic planning, less is more. People commonly make the mistake of chasing every opportunity that presents itself, as if they all offer the same potential benefit. View each strategic option as having a different value, and make sure you invest your time and energy wisely.

So, to narrow your options, place a value on each one. In our "starving actor" example (see Figure 6.3), he initially came up with 17

Figure 6.3. "Starving Actor" opportunity-based strategic plan for one positioning statement.

POSITIONING STATEMENTS	LONG-TERM GOALS	SHORT-TERM GOALS	BARRIERS TO ACHIEVING GOALS	STRATEGIC OPTIONS
To: My agent. I: Am an untapped potential for agency recognition, success, and income. Who: Can be presented to clients as a fresh, appealing talent. Because: I have proved my talent in several local productions and am a versatile and reliable actor.	Become a star on the big screen within 10 years.	Obtain a small part in a feature film within 24 months.	No feature film experience. Unknown commodity. Inattentive agent. Waning personal confidence after two years of failed attempts. Time is spent working for money as a waiter. Weak networking skills. Financially strapped.	Represent my short film experience. Shift to more upscale restaurant to earn more tips and higher salary. Hire a personal trainer to restore physically. Convince agent to be more attentive or change to an agent who specializes in young talent. Read *Variety* and proactively push agent for all roles, including TV commercials, corporate video shoots. Join local actors' group to meet others in field. Send out photos, videos, and letters to fresh agents likely to represent new faces. Investigate taking acting classes to gain more experience with different kinds of roles.

strategies to reach his short-term goals. He then went through the list and assigned a numerical value on each, and ended up selecting the top eight. You may be more comfortable keeping only the top three to five strategies.

To put this selection process into action, use the following two measures to rank your strategies (see Figure 6.4). A number from 1 to 3 reflects the impact on short-term goals while a letter from *A* to *C* shows your level of commitment to following each option. By ranking and judging the options, you will come up with the most potentially successful strategies. Your judgment of your situation will always be the arbiter. But should there be no discrepancies, a ranking of 1A has a very high probability of success, while a 3C ranking would seem to fall out of the selection process.

This ranking system directs your attention to the expected effects and personal dedication to the options. After all, it is foolish to sign on to a strategy that you don't really want to complete, even if it would have a high impact on reaching your short-term goals. But let's look at another example, this time one that could apply to many workers today. In fact, you may be in this exact situation with your employer, and you'll see that the ranking system is straightforward and relevant.

You will have more Brand YOU goals than you can handle strategies. Remember that appropriate strategies need to be devel-

Figure 6.4. Brand YOU strategic option rankings.

IMPACT ON SHORT-TERM GOAL	COMMITMENT TO FOLLOW THROUGH ON STRATEGY
1 Significant	A Significant
2 Medium	B Medium
3 Low	C Low

oped for each of your goals. Following this way of exploring your options will be eye-opening. Whether you are focusing on better fitness or financial success, developing your own strategic plans will improve the probability of your achieving those goals.

Susan's Ranking of Strategic Options

Susan has set a short-term goal of being promoted at work within 12 months, and she wants to explore the strategic options for achieving that goal. She has shortened her initial list of options as explained above, and has ranked the strongest two as follows:

- ➤ *1A*   Consider the possibility of relocation to another city if that is where the promotion opens up.
- ➤ *1A*   Volunteer to oversee a special project that will demonstrate my leadership of a team of four employees.

In this example, Susan has set a goal of earning a promotion within 12 months. One way she can help shape her strategy for achieving that goal would be to speak with a career counselor. While Susan has elected to meet with the Human Resources Manager at her company, she might choose to seek counsel from an outside recruiter to help her assess her current situation. By speaking with a professional, and being clear about her objective, she will gain an unbiased opinion of her potential success. This career recruiter may point out the skills required for a higher position; he will also have contacts in the industry and perhaps can recommend a weekend program for Susan to develop the skills needed. Susan has set her goals, ranked her strategies, and sought counsel before initiating any implementation of her strategies.

Imagine that you have set a personal short-term goal of becoming more financially secure. You currently have a monthly mortgage payment, car payments, utility bills, and bills for several credit cards that are at their maximum. Merely paying the service charge each month on those credit card balances has become a burden. You have set an important goal for yourself. While exploring your strategic options, you will want to consider the advice of a financial expert, and there are agencies that offer such assistance. Among your strategic options are steps to pay down your debts. Setting a realistic time line with incremental target dates will be necessary because this goal may take a few years to accomplish. However, the key is to weigh the options and get started on achieving the results you desire. That again brings us to implementation.

The implementation plan that follows in the wake of these strategies will be the final step in our 7 Steps to Creating Your Most Successful Self, and that is explained in the next chapter. For now, just think creatively about the best strategies for reaching your goals. Weigh all your options. Sometimes, your initial strategy choice may seem logical because it is comfortable. Upon further investigation, a more taxing strategy may be the best approach. Change is not easy and requires hard work and sacrifice.

Thus, identifying and understanding the many strategic options available to you is a critical step in determining your optimal strategies. These strategies are only as good as their ability to help you achieve your new Brand YOU goals. Since goals and strategies are so intertwined, be sure you have them aligned. This will pay off in the final step, implementation. But before we move on to that final step, let's take a look at Julie and see how she has handled the strategy stage of the process.

JULIE'S STRATEGIC OPTIONS

Julie is well into the 7 Steps process now. Having chosen her long- and short-term goals, she is ready to look at her strategic options. Let's look at Julie's worksheet (see Figure 6.5). (For the sake of brevity here, we've included only her Positioning Statement 1.)

Figure 6.5. Brand JULIE strategic planning worksheet.

POSITIONING STATEMENTS	LONG-TERM GOALS	SHORT-TERM GOALS	BARRIERS TO ACHIEVING GOALS	STRATEGIC OPTIONS
To: Me (Julie) I: Am a happy, centered, vibrant woman. Who: Is in complete control of my new life direction. Because: I have taken my passion for working with people and built a fresh and exciting career that allows me to fulfill my brand essence.	Ten years from now, at age 38, I will be a respected business leader who is impacting the lives of other people.	Pursue and achieve a bachelor's degree within 5 years. Build a personal system for being the top customer relations leader in the mall over the next 12 months. Reenter the theater over the next 12 months.	Current requirements of my job. Potential financial barrier of cost of college. Lack of knowledge of contemporary customer systems. Lack of current connection of any theater group. A general concern over time requirement and potential cost.	Gather the facts regarding college admission requirements and financial aid ASAP. Learn how professional CRM (Customer Relationship Management) systems work. Determine the data management systems I should consider learning. Work to improve my customer interviewing skills. Join a local theater group; join a local health club. Return to childhood church. Look into her current banking services for strategic guidance.

Julie took into account her long- and short-term goals as she identified her strategic options. With so many options listed, she had to reconsider them and refer back to her time balance grid to ascertain if she had the available time for so many strategies. For example, she had concluded that the local YMCA was her best choice for fitness work. This is a natural tendency, since convenient location is immediately appealing; however, now she realizes there are more options to contemplate. Even her decision to go to college presents complicated choices. After all, Julie has been out of high school for over 10 years, and her application to college represents a nontraditional admission; also, a full class schedule may make other options difficult to pursue. She remains committed to her goals, but appreciates the need to be more methodical in tracing her personal roadmap.

Julie uses the ranking system to classify the key alternatives, based on their impact and her personal commitment to follow through on implementation. Let's look at how she ranked her strategic options.

> *1A* Gather all facts regarding college.
> *1A* Learn about CRM systems.
> *1C* Join a local health club.
> *1C* Join a local theater group.
> *2A*
> *2B*
> *2C* Return to childhood church.
> *3A* Look into current banking services for strategic guidance.
> *3B*
> *3C*

Julie completes her ranking of strategic options and is a bit overwhelmed. As she developed her goals earlier, she felt committed to each one, yet as this step has pointed out, she has varying commitments to implementing them. This is not to suggest that one goal is less important to Julie than another. However, it does show her the reality: if she is to accomplish her goals, she will need an iron-clad plan of action because she is prone to settle back and accept her status quo.

This is when Julie's 10-year long-term goal shines like a beacon of light on the path for her: "Ten years from now, at age 38, I will be a respected business leader who is impacting the lives of other people." She knows she wants to achieve this goal, yet the realization that she is already losing focus is a wake-up call. She has come so far in her journey to become the Brand JULIE she wants to create. Now she realizes how important the final step, implementation, is going to be. Without an action plan to follow with pride and confidence, her work is in jeopardy. In fact, she reminds herself of the many other times she said, "I am going to go back to school, become an even better advisor to my customers, and improve my overall well-being." However, this time, she vows to commit to repositioning her Brand JULIE and achieving her goals.

CHAPTER 7

I AM READY TO COMMIT TO MY ACTION PLAN

STEP SEVEN: IMPLEMENT, MONITOR, AND ADJUST YOUR NEW BRAND **YOU**

"Action speaks louder than words, but not nearly as often."
—MARK TWAIN

AS ONE JOURNEY ENDS, so another begins. You have assessed your current life and have a commitment to build a new Brand YOU. This has taken honesty, perseverance, and conviction. Yet, you still have only pieces of a plan. Now is the time to bring the elements together and make a plan that will happen. This step is the implementation phase, which additionally includes the important tasks of monitoring and adjustment.

A vision without action is just a fantasy. Everyday, around the world, picture-perfect brand positioning strategies are put to the test. Winning or losing with consumers—it all comes down to how

well a strategy is executed and how well the message reaches the hearts, minds, and pocketbooks of consumers. The best plans in the world, poorly implemented, fall flat. An average plan, executed flawlessly, beats a more profound plan that is not put into operation. Just as every play in a football coach's playbook is designed to yield a touchdown, every strategy supported by lists of tactics is designed to succeed. Obviously, they don't always do that, and the reason they don't succeed has little to do with the plan and lots to do with the implementation.

A vision without action is just a fantasy.

THE PRINCIPLES OF SUCCESSFUL IMPLEMENTATION

Successful implementation requires an attention to detail, frequent reality checks, and unwavering commitment. Otherwise, the energy that has been put into building a strategic plan will be wasted. So, a lot is riding on this final step in the process.

There is no shortage of ideas, information, theories, and strategies. Unfortunately, too often there is a shortage of commitment. Flawed implementation is why plans fail, strategies flounder, and companies, products, and individuals struggle to survive. Everything in life is 5 percent idea and 95 percent implementation, to modify Thomas Edison's famous quip just a little.

Hundreds of millions of dollars are spent annually to influence you to buy particular brands of soft drinks, pizzas, automobiles,

clothing, computers, or insurance. Companies take time and use the best intelligence available to construct winning positions in the market, set achievable goals, and develop effective strategies. All start the year with the intention of winning sales from their target consumers at the point of purchase and having a banner year. The point that separates success and failure is generally found in the planning process and the execution activities. Implementation is a discipline unto itself, and significant attention must be paid to this activity.

Everything in life is 5 percent idea and
95 percent implementation.

Many companies stake their reputation on the ability to execute a "brand promise," with effective "brand positioning." As an example, FedEx focuses on flawless execution as an aspect of its corporate culture, taking implementation seriously. This corporation recognizes the power in delivering on its promise: "Absolutely Positively." While this is an old tag line from a previous marketing campaign, it still represents the mindset of this organization. In 2007, *Fortune* magazine ranked FedEx number seven among the World's Most Admired Companies.

Daily, thorough implementation by more than 280,000 employees worldwide makes FedEx a leader. Yet, FedEx's leadership position didn't happen by accident. FedEx is organized to win and dedicated to executing its promise in more than 220 countries and territories. In fact, during 2006, FedEx successfully completed 6.5 million shipments on an average day, utilizing 609 aircraft, 75,000 motorized vehicles, and 375 airports. With hand-held technology and world-class

routing systems, FedEx has a distribution chain with people able to fulfill all their responsibilities, extending even to being able to modify delivery schedules based on weather and traffic conditions.

Such systemic commitment to excellence in implementation has resulted in a global consumer base. FedEx understands its obligation to deliver goods on a timely basis and has built the systems, processes, and disciplines to ensure consumer satisfaction and brand loyalty. In short, they are a stellar brand because of stellar implementation.

FIVE FACTORS FOR SUCCESSFUL IMPLEMENTATION

Your personal branding success will also not happen by accident. There are five essential factors that ensure the highest level of implementation, whether by a company or by you in your quest for a new Brand YOU.

1. Clear objectives have been established.
2. People have been given responsibility for implementation. (In the case of Brand YOU, that means you.)
3. Expectations are in place and well understood by those who are accountable.
4. Performance is monitored regularly.
5. The strategy is flexible enough to accommodate adjustments during implementation.

Successful companies follow these five principles to improve the delivery of their brand promise to target consumers. Remember,

the work of brand building does not end when the product is made, advertised, and shipped. Implementation goes all the way to the point of purchase and even to use of the brand by consumers. Failure to think of the retailing obligation leaves the success of brand positioning to chance. The brands that earn consumer loyalty have assigned great time and resources to detailed implementation systems.

For many categories of products, companies rely on retail centers to bring their brands to life with the consumers. This is especially true of durable goods such as cars, washers and dryers, computers, and lawn equipment, as some examples. Consider the young adult who has decided to purchase his first new car. He's been driving a used car for years, and now that his career is in full swing, he decides to upgrade to a new car. After conducting the due diligence, he narrows the selection to four manufacturers. The four companies offer similar size models with similar features and are priced in the same range. However, one model is his personal choice for its sportier look. He feels it would be more fun to drive, at the same time safer and more reliable; in essence, the model fits his new lifestyle and projects the identity consistent with his new personal brand.

Off this eager shopper goes to test-drive all four models. As he enters the dealership, he really enters each brand. The showrooms have different feels and provide different customer experiences. At the first dealership, this prospective buyer is greeted promptly by a sales agent who appears friendly, takes the young man seriously as a prospect, shows the display model on the floor, and offers a test drive. He feels no undue pressure to make a decision, and he likes the car and sales representative. Even though this particular car model had been his last choice among the four, it is now a serious consideration.

The good feeling quickly changes when he enters the second dealership, which happened to have his first-choice model of car. But in the showroom, he detects a general lack of interest, as well as a lack of respect for him as a buyer; also, he finds out there is limited inventory of this model and the sales rep appears unfamiliar with the car's options. Nevertheless, the sales rep tries to push him to make a decision today or risk losing a "good deal." Thus, in a few short minutes, this auto manufacturer fell from a position of brand insistence to one of disdain, all because of the retail outlet's environment, lack of receptivity, and indifferent attitude.

Poor implementation can negate the consumer's image of even the best product. This car shopping example occurs all the time. Successful manufacturers have a responsibility to make sure their retailers deliver the brand promise consistently. Otherwise, shoppers will go wherever else they receive proper attention and good customer service. This is why many franchise brands have explicit operating standards that must be maintained in order to hold the franchise rights. Key to this situation, of course, is the need for monitoring the maintenance of those standards. As the old adage goes, "Inspect what you expect."

Poor implementation can negate the consumer's image of even the best product.

THE BEST OF INTENTIONS
WON'T DO IT

Successful implementation of your new Brand YOU positioning strategies requires your concentration on this point. Remember, the environment around you—your demeanor, your attitude, your responsiveness to the needs of others, your attention to detail—all can negatively impact others' perceptions of your personal brand. So, think of implementation as a discipline unto itself and your commitment to implementation with distinction as a way to separate you from the pack. Many people talk about transforming their lives, to laying down good plans, but then they stumble before reaching the finish line. Why? They fail to implement and execute!

Every January, well-intentioned people undertake the physical fitness journey. That is, equipped with their New Year's resolutions to become healthier, they buy the gym clothes and club membership and then off they go. January is a great month for turning over a new leaf, for making important resolutions, for reinventing yourself. New gym memberships soar; people converge on treadmills, weight machines, stationary bicycles, and indoor tracks. As the months go by, and the muscles get tired, the treadmill lines subside and the new members dwindle; people have moved back into their ruts. The bikes worked fine. The weights were set properly. The fitness instructors were at their places, the work-out music was blasting. It's not the plan that failed—it was the implementation. Or, in this case, chalk it up to lack of discipline in the implementation phase.

Implementation matters, yet it generally does not get the same level of focus as the brand positioning and strategy work. As we've shown, in business great execution is the differentiation

point for many brands. It can also be the differentiation point for the new Brand YOU.

BRAND YOU IMPLEMENTATION GUIDELINES

Throughout the 7 Steps to Creating Your Most Successful Self, you have been introduced to many facets of business brand management and been shown how to apply those facets to your personal brand. As you can see from our discussion above, there are elements of implementation that merit your special attention, too. Including the five factors in your personal strategic implementation plan will bring proper focus to your effort.

Personal Commitment

Commitment to your strategic plan is essential if you want to successfully establish the new Brand YOU. You must make a personal promise to achieve the goals you have identified. The implementation plan includes the what, when, where, who, and how that will bring your strategies to life. But this means putting those new activities on your calendar and then doing them. This will take courage; after all, your new activities will mean being with different people in unfamiliar situations. While the temptation may be to retreat to your comfort zone, be confident in your future. You have completed the due diligence of the first six steps. That should strengthen your fortitude to continue.

Do not underestimate the distraction factor. We are so busy, rich in activities and poor in time; we sometimes "table" our goals and

postpone doing those things we've decided were vital and important. Don't be distracted. Don't waiver. Remember, you need to focus on your new Brand YOU as if your life depended on it. Why? Because it does!

This implementation step is often where things break down. Whether it's that your schedule is too hectic, or you just have lost the passion, these are derailers and you should be alert to them. Nike has its slogan, "Just Do It!" What do you have to lose? Any personal reward comes as the result of risk. Instead, let small victories be the motivation to propel you forward. Legendary hockey player Wayne Gretzky said, "I miss 100 percent of the shots I never take." Go for it!

Confidence grows with learning from small steps. Taking small steps minimizes the personal jeopardy and lets you know when you are doing too much or too little. You can determine the right mix of personal risk and personal comfort. After all, as you learned during the Brand YOU audit, you are a function of everything that has happened in your life up to this point, so some things will be easier than others.

Just as small victories can boost confidence, small setbacks can cause you to question your resolve. View all of your attempts as learning opportunities. After all, if you weren't trying new things, you wouldn't be challenging yourself. Monitor your progress, and adjust your plans as you gain insights.

Stay the Course

Suppose you are going to implement your strategy of broadening your network beyond your condo complex friends. This strategy makes great sense on paper, and now you are about to step into a world of new people and new relationships. As a start, you will

visit a local museum and study the paintings and sculptures. You select the museum, find the parking lot, and mingle with strangers in the galleries. But upon arrival, you are confused by the large parking lot, wind up in a long line to buy your ticket, and can't stand the contemporary art exhibited. You meet a few people, but only for a brief hello. On the way out, you pick up a flyer listing upcoming events and you retreat to your car. This is the moment of truth.

You have had a new experience that turned out to be unfulfilling and the effort has left you disappointed. Still, don't drop your commitment to your strategy. While you may have felt awkward, nobody else knew of your concerns. You learned about art museums, you made it through the galleries of art you couldn't appreciate, and now you know more than you did before. If this was a totally miserable experience, you may want to choose another activity that will bring you into more contact with new people. However, now you know where to park, and have the schedule of upcoming events. You also found out you can buy the tickets in advance online. In fact, as you review the calendar of events, you see some exhibitions that could be enjoyable.

So, while your initial reaction was negative, you are primed for a second try. This time you will have a better feel for the situation and higher personal confidence. In any event, don't become the victim of your own negativity. Take another trip with greater confidence this time. Be positive with those around you, and see the positive aspects of new experiences; most important, be positive to yourself. You have every reason to be confident in your implementation plans, so when something new is not quite what you expected, accept the learning experience, regroup, return, and rebound. Life is not a straight line; it's a series of ups, downs, and sideways.

THE BRAND YOU ACTION PLAN

Implementation requires detailed plans. Begin those plans with a calendar of your scheduled actions. A simple Brand YOU action plan worksheet (see Figure 7.1) will set you in motion. Using your ranking of strategic priorities done in Chapter 6, plot a three- to six-month calendar based on the when, what, where, how, and who of what you'll be doing. The entries should be concise but complete enough to state what will be accomplished.

Details really matter here. Even if you are prepared for a new activity, but have incorrect directions to the location, your Brand YOU plan can be derailed. A three- to six-month period is best because this length of time gives you opportunities to plan many different activities. As an example, if you begin jogging as an activity, you may want to sign up for a "fun run" four months away. Preparing for this run becomes a short-term goal and a rallying cry that can keep you on track.

Remember, each objective should contribute to your new brand identity and help with your brand positioning. Here are a few tips to help get you started:

➤ *Brand Image Enhancement.* Have a couple of full-length photographs taken of you showing your front, back, and side. Then, notice your appearance, posture, clothing. Do these photographs show a person who is consistent with your positioning statements? Stand in front of a mirror and speak for a couple of minutes. Notice how you hold your head, move your mouth, and use your facial expressions to convey meaning. Record your voice on a tape recorder and listen to how you sound reading a paragraph aloud. Or, record your voice during a telephone conversation (be sure to inform the person on the other end that you are recording).

Figure 7.1. Brand YOU action plan worksheet.

WHEN	WHAT	WHERE	HOW	WHO
[Date] [Time]	[Activity]	[Location, in-cluding travel time]	[Preparation, if any]	[Key contacts, including phone numbers, e-mail]

➤ *Brand Identity Enhancement.* Go to your closet and look at your clothes. Do you have the basic elements that contribute to the identity you want? How well do you take care of yourself relative to your overall appearance? While remaining true to yourself, realize that everything communicates your identity to others, including your appearance. In the past six months, have you spent time with people in activities that support the identity you want? Look around your home or place of employment. Does it project the identity you would like? Are you on time when meeting others, prepared, trustworthy, kind, cheerful? How do you represent yourself around others?

➤ *Brand Personality Enhancement.* Look at your bookcase, DVD or CD collection, or songs on your MP3 player. These are a reflection of your personality. Is there a broad array of artists and authors, or a narrow band of interest? What pictures hang on your walls? Your choice of visual stimulation reflects your personality and may be a peek into your brand essence.

➤ *Brand Essence Enhancement.* What television shows or movies do you absolutely love? What is the most important characteristic you look for in a friend? What historical or contemporary people do you admire, and why? These favorites provide insight into what constitutes your heart and soul. What words from others have struck a chord with you? What actions have you observed of others that have motivated you? What physical locations do you find most satisfying? How do you achieve tranquility or peace of mind? What soothes or inspires you is indicative of your very essence.

With your action plan in hand, you begin to implement your strategies. But as this is a long process, you'll need to monitor your progress and adjust your strategies accordingly.

MONITORING AND ADJUSTMENT

Even the best-laid plans need some modification along the way. Change is good. Adaptation is great. In the case of FedEx, which we spoke of earlier in the chapter, storms appear regularly that require frontline employees and drivers to alter delivery schedules, thereby adapting to changing conditions. Albert Einstein defined *insanity* as doing the same thing over and over and expecting different results. So don't be afraid of shifting gears to accommodate different conditions.

Along the way, you will want to and need to alter your strategy for implementation. These course corrections should be driven by actions that have produced a new perspective on your plans. You may also determine that your learning has shifted your thoughts, and a different tactic would be more successful in the short or long run. Regardless of the reason, be prepared to adjust your actions at some point. Even when your schedule is going great, feel that you can add or delete activities as you see fit.

These modifications in implementation represent decisions you have made to enhance the process. In other words, deleting activities from your calendar because you've lost interest in the process is not acceptable. However, occasionally things will come up that deserve special consideration, and perhaps alteration, for the right reasons. Being nimble at this stage will help you avoid getting trapped in a rigid plan.

Your best friend in the implementation stage is your action plan. Put the activities on your calendar and hold yourself accountable to complete them and track your progress. You will be amazed at how effectively a five-minute daily routine can keep you on track. You should have scheduled activities every week, and your days should begin with a review of your plan. While no imple-

mentation plan can be complete, you can ensure that it includes your key activities far enough into the future. Remember, thorough implementation ensures success for your strategic plan, which supports your short- and long-term goals.

JULIE IMPLEMENTS HER PLAN

Julie sits down to do the final step in the 7 Steps to Creating Your Most Successful Self process with a true sense of purpose. She has determined to take control of her life, in spite of previous failed attempts. "This time," she exclaims, "will be different!" I "have tried things in the past randomly and sometimes in pursuit of the latest fad. I have never had a customized plan that will reposition me," she thought. So, she reviewed her documents, including her list of short-term goals and her strategic plan, including her ranking of strategic priorities, and began to chart her activities for the next few weeks and months.

Julie realizes she might be tempted to bite off more than she can chew at this early stage of implementation, but has chosen to err on the side of aggressive action rather than take a passive stance. After all, she surmises, "I can always back off a little bit, but I am ready and eager to transform my life." So, off she goes, to build her action plan, based on her strategic planning worksheet (Figure 6.5).

It is Sunday afternoon, February 1, and she completes her action plan (see Figure 7.2) based on the worksheet presented earlier in this chapter.

Julie feels great about this commitment schedule and is eager to implement her action plan. But as the proof is in the pudding,

Figure 7.2. Brand JULIE action plan.

WHEN	WHAT	WHERE	HOW	WHO
2/1	Write and commit to action plan.			Julie
2/3 in the AM	On her day off, go to the local university and junior college and gather information for admissions.	On campus	No appointment. General information gathering. Business casual attire.	Julie
2/3 in the PM	Visit YMCA and two other gyms to see what programs they offer.	Near home or work	Drop by.	Julie
2/6 during lunch break	Go to bookstore and look for easy guide to customer management systems.	Mall where she works		
2/7 AM	Go to new church of her faith.	Church near her apartment	"Sunday" attire.	Julie
2/7 PM	Organize her thinking on the college situation.	In her apartment	By appt. in business casual attire.	
2/10 AM	Meet with banking planner to discuss personal financial goals and situation.	At the bank		
By 2/28	Look into theater opportunities.	Weekly magazines, online		
By 3/10	Begin my new customer management program.	Implement the tools and techniques learned in the manuals	At work, in an updated business professional look.	Julie with her top clients
By 3/15	Decide on college.			Julie with her mother, college counselor, and manager at work
By 4/1	Be well into workout program.	At gym with new people	Following the advice of a personal trainer.	Gym team with newfound friends
By 9/15	Enter college.	To be determined		
By 12/31	Be involved in theater in community.	To be determined		
By 12/31	Have my customer relationship system implemented with at least my top 25 clients.			

let's look ahead at how well Julie has succeeded in keeping her commitments.

Julie, Two Years Later

Two years into her repositioning, Julie has been vigilant keeping to her plan and is still executing it. She has faced some challenges but her Brand JULIE approach has kept her on a path that is already delivering results.

For example, Julie found that the local university was less than helpful in her quest for a degree. Her high school transcript showed her grades as well below the required GPA and her SAT scores were also below standard. Normally, this news would have been enough to send Julie back into her rut, but since she had several strategic options, she remained committed to her vision of obtaining a college degree. After consulting with her mother (adult to adult, mom as trusted advisor), Julie decided to pursue junior college. She found the admissions department at the local community college to be more understanding of her nontraditional status, and in spite of her poor grades and SAT score, Julie was accepted as a freshman. She got started during the summer semester, giving her a jump-start on her mission to earn her degree. The heavy course load put a strain on her work obligations, and she had not qualified for any financial aid, so pressures did mount during the first few months, but she persevered.

Prior to starting college, Julie had also found a simple process that would help build her client skills. In fact, she no longer thought of herself as an assistant manager selling to customers, but as a leader of the customers who had developed brand insistence for her services. She went to the local hair and beauty salon and got an image makeover—nothing too dramatic, but an updated look to go

along with her updated professional business woman identity. She was amazed at how well she was able to anticipate the needs of her 25 clients, just based on this new system. She could now reach them in advance of new shipments, set up private wardrobe showings, and meet all their apparel needs. The clients loved this personal attention, and Julie's sales were up 30 percent. People in the store were noticing a major difference in Julie—a major difference that was, by the way, all positive.

As Julie investigated the different gyms and fitness clubs in her area, she was amazed at the prices and atmosphere. To her, none of these clubs fit her "brand essence," in the sense that some seemed to be socializing spots while others felt like a male-dominated weight room. This was a big disappointment, and she was unwilling to spend her hard-earned money in a place that went against her principles. She did start exercising in the basement gym of her local church, which she started to attend—even though, at first, this kind of socializing was a bit peculiar. Since her attendance as an adult had been infrequent, her first two services were awkward. However, consistent with her Brand JULIE plan, she continued to go. On the third week, something about the situation seemed to click with her, and she met a couple of people her age. They invited her to join them for lunch and at that lunch they introduced her to friends who, since then, have grown close. And, to boot, the church's fitness program was free to members; after reading a self-help book on training, she developed her own workout program and is now well on her way to being a healthier, more fit Julie.

The best thing about the church experience is that she has met a nice guy who is also divorced and has a young child. They have been dating for a few months now. He is a college graduate and has helped her with her studies. While Julie is taking this relationship slowly, she is happy with her newfound love interest.

An interesting thing happened to Julie at work about 18 months into this plan. One of her clients approached her to learn more about her unique customer service system. This woman was a successful businessperson who owned her own company and was in consulting. Her business was expanding, and she offered Julie a job as Director of Training and Development, owing to her extraordinary client services skills. Julie was astounded by this opportunity, but volunteered that she did not have her college degree yet and indicated that she was attending the local junior college. This CEO was so impressed with her honesty that she said she would make an exception to her basic rule of not hiring people lacking college degrees, and that her company benefits plan included tuition reimbursement, which she would qualify for. Julie took this job and left the department store, much to her dismay. She had not been looking for a new job, but since this came her way, she decided to make the move. Once again, her mother proved to give sound advice during this difficult decision; so did her boyfriend.

With a year's academic study under her belt, Julie applied to transfer to the four-year college that had snubbed her earlier. With her accumulated credits, her solid college GPA, and glowing recommendations from her CEO, she was accepted into the bachelor's degree program.

Also, Julie is planning to move into a nicer apartment that is closer to her work and the college. As for her theater plans, well, this option did not materialize. But that's not bad, given that Julie has made such progress in every other category. She looked into the theater option early on, but wasn't impressed with the local group. With everything else going well for her, she didn't regret this "missed target." And, she has noticed that the college has a small theater club, so this option may be back in her plan in the future.

Only time will tell where Julie will take her life, her new brand,

and her future. She has aggressively repositioned herself and she is well on her way to realizing her 10-year vision. She achieved her positioning statements so well that someone in her target audience hired her for her very own leadership team. That is the ultimate compliment.

Julie's personal life is blossoming because she made the tough decision to focus and sacrifice, just as corporate brands do to be successful. Nevertheless, she has remained true to herself. All in all, Julie is a great example of someone who has learned to *manage Brand YOU*.

COMMENCEMENT

"Action is the foundational key to all success."
—PABLO PICASSO

CONGRATULATIONS! CONGRATULATIONS on your dedication, perseverance, and belief in yourself. Through your personal commitment to the 7 Steps to Creating Your Most Successful Self, you are now in control of the development of your personal brand. Regardless of what life throws your way, you can reinvent, restage, and reposition yourself, yet remain true to your core principles. By applying the techniques successfully pursued by businesses, you've built a new brand identity that inspires brand loyalty. Your role models have been high-profile individuals, leading corporations, and a few fictional characters such as Roger and Julie. You've received their ideas, tips, guidelines, methods, and, we hope, inspiration.

Remember, though, that your new Brand YOU is a work in progress; just because you have a plan and the plan seems to be working, don't take your eye off the ball. The one constant in life is change. You'll constantly be confronting new situations that demand decisions on your part. Questions will arise, such as, "How will I position myself in this world of mixed messages and frantic

timelines?" and "How do I stand out in a crowd, and remain true to myself?" The Brand YOU process is repeatable, continuous, and worthy of revisiting when things dramatically change in your life—or when you're ready to dramatically change your life again. You should constantly monitor your brand's health. After all, unpoliced brands lose their value. Focus on continuous improvement, and plan your life to work your plan.

This process was not intended to provide a quickie makeover. The book was born of some great branding best practices in the business world and was crafted to serve individuals with the belief that people are as much brands as are corporations, products, and services. It is our hope that you will find in these pages the help you are seeking in making changes in your life.

You should be proud of your dedication to personal improvement. In the spirit of *Managing Brand YOU*, we wish you well on your personal journey. Should you wish to tell us of your experience, we can be contacted at www.managingbrandyou.com.

GLOSSARY OF BRANDING TERMS

HERE IS A QUICK-PASS GLOSSARY of the terms that are used most frequently by branding professionals, and that are used in this book. After all, if you are to become a successful Brand YOU manager, you need to understand these terms.

BRAND ATTRIBUTES represent the associations that are attached to a brand. They could represent physical or emotional associations. Different individuals may see different brand attributes in a product or a service or a personal brand for that matter. Attribute relevancy is often in the eyes of the beholder.

BRAND AUDIT is the MRI or CT Scan or X-Ray or "Lab Work" of the branding world. It represents the complete diagnostic, analysis, and evaluation of a brand from top to bottom. From logo, symbol, colors, positioning, target audiences, relevancy, message, awareness, satisfaction, scores, and more . . . it is the activity associated with a brand taking stock in itself so it can ultimately improve and enhance its effectiveness.

BRAND AWARENESS (also called *brand recall*) is the measure of familiarity customers have with a brand. *Aided brand awareness* is when customers are given hints about a brand to help them recall the brand. In the case of personal branding, imagine yourself at a party. You see someone across the crowded room, but can't remember his name. When you ask a companion for help, she says "You re-

member John, don't you? He's the guy who used to be on the school board and lives in the same cul de sac as the Smiths." That's an example of aided brand awareness. Without assistance, you wouldn't recall John. *Unaided brand awareness* simply means that customers recognize a brand without assistance and without hints. And so, even a 3-year-old child who doesn't read can recognize the "golden arches" of McDonald's from a distance! That is an example of how a brand symbol conveys the brand. In the case of personal branding, unaided brand awareness is said to be "top of the mind." Don't ever forget that it's better to be remembered than to be recalled.

BRAND BENEFIT is the positive effect a brand delivers and provides. Brand benefits may be functional, as with a vehicle that you can drive from home to school and back. These are basic benefits that are easily copied by competitors. However, emotional benefits of a brand could include how you feel when you drive your vehicle. If you are proud of your car and it reflects your personality, this bonds you to the brand better than do functional benefits. For personal branding, think about your closest friend. He is a brand who provides you the benefits of love, compassion, understanding, companionship, counsel, and so on. Those are all brand benefits that represent a value to the end user.

BRAND EQUITY represents the assets linked to a brand, which add up to the perceived value provided by that brand. In terms of personal branding, we hope that our personal brand equity includes assets such as reliability, trustworthiness, integrity, honesty, great sense of humor, kindness, empathy, sympathy, character, and competency. Equities are transferable to other parts of our life and should be treated as personal strengths. They are positive features or skills you have developed over the years. Needless to say, just as financial

wealth and economic health are directly correlated to your material assets, your personal brand wealth and health are a reflection of your brand assets.

BRAND ESSENCE is the core of a brand's identity and it defines what a brand stands for or represents to others. Think of brand essence as the heart and soul of the brand. These inner values should never be compromised. For example, Hallmark Cards markets its products under the slogan, "When You Care Enough to Send the Very Best." Hallmark's brand essence, then, is that its products are "the very best."

BRAND IDENTITY is how a strategist wants a brand to be perceived by the various target audiences. Brand identity is thoughtfully developed after the strategic, or *brand, intent* is defined. Successful brands identify what they want to stand for and have a plan to bring that vision to life. While brand image is the overall perception, brand identity symbolizes what the brand wants to be known for. In personal branding, it's what you want others to think about you when you walk into a room.

BRAND IMAGE is how customers perceive the brand. It may differ from *brand intent* (the way the company would like its brand to be perceived) but comes through others' eyes. Think of brand image as the total perception customers have of a brand. With respect to personal branding, brand image is how others think of you. This is a compilation of the thoughts and images people have of you today. Needless to say, some of these images might have been years in the making and are based on past interactions with you. While you may not agree with these observations, they are real as perceptions in the minds of those around you. Like it or not, the perspective of others defines your brand.

BRAND INSISTENCE is the strong position consumers take on purchasing the brand of their choice. An example is the woman who goes to a drugstore seeking Paul Mitchell hair-care products and will not buy another brand when her choice is out of stock. In personal branding, wouldn't it be wonderful if your employer insisted that you were the only person for the promotion? Brand insistence means unwavering commitment to a specific brand.

BRAND INTENT. See *brand identity*.

BRAND LOYALTY is the consistent repurchase of a brand. In the case of personal branding, it may very well be how loyal others are to you. However, when customers' favorite brand is not readily available, they may select another brand. While business brands desire loyalty and work to earn this, there are always competing factors, such as convenience. Imagine that you want a cup of coffee; though you are generally loyal to Starbucks, you stop in another coffee shop because it is more convenient—for this occasion a substitute shop is fine. Though it would be flattering if an important client meeting was postponed because you were unavailable, other considerations sometimes dictate exceptions to personal brand loyalty as well.

BRAND PERSONALITY simply put, is assigning human personality traits to a brand. Where this is common practice with products and services (e.g., "a company with a heart . . . " "a service that listens to its customers well . . . " "a store that is always warm, friendly, and helpful . . . "), when discussing personal branding, it represents the key personality traits associated with an individual (e.g., cerebral, impulsive, witty, empathetic, etc.).

BRAND POSITIONING is a mapping strategy based on the market space a product, service, or company is slated to occupy. In per-

sonal branding, positioning refers to the specific group of people an individual brand targets, and whose hearts and minds really matter. Positioning categorizes a brand. Just as a consumer brand can be "positioned" as high quality, average, or even "low end," so can people be categorized similarly. Positioning a personal brand is simply placing an individual in the space he or she cares to occupy.

BRAND PREFERENCE exists when a consumer would rather choose one brand over another when there's a choice. In personal branding, we all want to be the brand of choice, whether it is for friendship or leadership. Being the PTA candidate of choice to lead the high school booster club is an example brand preference.

BRAND RECALL. See *brand awareness.*

BRAND REJECTION comes about when a consumer or customer is so well committed to another brand that they rarely will give a competing brand a try. An example of this is a loyal Coca-Cola customer who, on an airplane, is offered Pepsi because a specific airline is on a Pepsi contract. Refusing to drink the Pepsi and requesting a juice in its place is an example of "brand rejection."

CORE ESSENCE is the basic foundation and positioning of a brand's promise in the simplest terms. It is the heart and soul of a brand. In an individual, it very well could be the heart, soul, and DNA of a personal brand. It is the one core characteristic that defines a product, service, company, or individual. Just as the core essence of a product could be "reliability" and a company's core essence could be its "community focus," an individual's core essence could very well be "integrity."

FRAME OF REFERENCE is a term that describes one's perspective. It takes into consideration one's history and experience base, and

uses those experiences as filters to define right or wrong . . . good or bad . . . success or failure. Although it is sometimes highly subjective, we all define things through our own personal points-of-view, perspective, and "frame of reference."

PASSION POINT is an expression that describes an activity, an event, and an emotion that represents the height of an individual's excitement, love, and support for an activity or experience. A passion point could be the feeling of accomplishment after one achieves a difficult task . . . or it could be the feeling of satisfaction (and relief) after one has an epiphany. It is an overarching feeling of jubilation and excitement.

POINT OF DIFFERENCE Brands diligently work to achieve a discernible, sustainable point of difference. Sometimes called "the unique attribute," or the "wow factor," or the "famous factor," this is what sets a brand (a product, a service, or a person) apart from others.

TARGET AUDIENCE represents the logical group a brand's message is directed toward. Once a target audience or audiences is or are defined, all communication to that target should be both harmonious and consistent . . . and well positioned for the target. Quick service giant Burger King's brand is focused and targeted to an audience they call their "super fans." A Burger King super fan is an 18-34 year old male who is likely to order a Whopper, large fries and an "upsized" Coca-Cola (not Diet Coke). He is typically an NFL or NHL fan who is likely to also be a NASCAR fan as well.

INDEX

childhood, 38–39
co-branding, 94
Coca-Cola Company, 6–7, 117
*The Collected Autobiographies
    of Maya Angelou* (Maya
    Angelou), 45
commitment, 204–206
consistency, 6, 21, 118, 127
consumer experience, 10, 11, 16–17,
    20
Consumer Reports, 94
consumer segmentation analyses,
    109–110
continuity, 21
core essence, 155–156
creative visualization, 106
credibility, 126
customer loyalty, 14, 126
customer perceptions, 11–14

differentiation, 182
dislikes, discovering, 86–89
Disney, *see* Walt Disney Company
Disney, Roy, 63
Disney, Walt, 62–64
Disneyland Park, 63
Doran, George T., 161
dreams, 165
Drucker, Peter F.
    on creating your future, 1, 5
    on strategy, 178

eBay, 11–12
Edison, Thomas, on genius, 30
education, 182–183
Einstein, Albert, on insanity, 210
"elevator discussion," 144
Eliot, T. S., on understanding
    ourselves, 33
emotions, 22, 112
endorsements, 79

equity
    brand, 80–84
    personal, 77
    transferable, 79
experience(s)
    consumer, 10, 11, 16–17, 20
    life, 48
    past, 34–35, 43–45

Fairmont, 22
"Faust" (Johann Wolfgang von
    Goethe), 42
FedEx, 118, 199–200, 210
feedback, 61, 66–70
flexibility, 165–166
focus, 23, 119
Fortune magazine, 199
Four Seasons Hotels and Resorts,
    23
frame of reference, 138–140, 143,
    146
franchises, 202
Franklin, Benjamin, 30
    as CEO of Pennsylvania, 42
    on pain and gain, 29

Gandhi, Mohandas "Mahatma,"
    64–66
gaps, 80–86
    correcting, 84–86
    identifying, 80–82
    overcompensating for, 83–84
    weaknesses vs., 80
Gather Together in My Name (Maya
    Angelou), 45
goal setting, 153–176
    Julie as example of, 170–176
    and personal priorities,
        155–160
    SMART, 161–169
Goethe, Johann Wolfgang von, 42

ABOUT THE AUTHORS

JERRY S. WILSON

For over three decades, Jerry has distinguished himself as a business leader who is committed to success through his focus on people development. This skill combined with his expertise in strategic planning, brand management, customer value creation, and operational execution has delivered significant results throughout his extensive career in the field of consumer goods.

Jerry is a board-elected Senior Vice President of The Coca-Cola Company, where he currently serves as President of the Global McDonald's Division. In his executive role, he is responsible for enhancing this strategic alliance through leadership marketing and operational excellence. He leads a corporate center and cross functional business units in the United States, Canada, Latin America, Asia Pacific, and Europe/Eurasia/Middle East/Africa. This worldwide responsibility spans 120 countries and over 32,000 restaurants. Jerry is also a member of the company's senior leadership team, which sets business strategy and operating goals.

During his twenty years with Coca-Cola, Jerry has risen from an area account executive, to regional management, to Strategic Brand and Planning Director, to Vice President of Western USA Foodservice. Prior to his current position, he served within the McDonald's Division as Vice President of USA Operations, and Global Chief Operating Officer.

Before, his career with Coke, Jerry spent over eight years in the automobile industry with Volkswagen of America, where he held a variety of positions. He joined the company as a distribution analyst, moved up to district sales manager, and then was developed through business management, sales training, marketing management, and franchise management responsibilities. Jerry was then promoted to Brand Manager for the USA, where he was responsible for developing strategies while liaising with the franchise leadership and company worldwide headquarters in Wolfsburg, Germany.

Jerry earned his MBA in Marketing from Mercer University, and his B.A. in Economics from the University of Georgia.

Jerry is an open-minded person who believes everyone has something to offer to this world and that no book should be judged by its cover. He has mentored many people over the years, and operates with an open-door policy so that all voices may be heard. He also believes people should find their inner passion and play to this personal space rather than settle for what happens to come their way.

Jerry has worked his way up from "surviving" to "thriving" and is always mindful of his journey, the people who believed in him along the way, and the fragility of life. In the mere blink of an eye, life can take an unexpected turn. Therefore, Jerry tries to make the most of every single day, live with an optimistic attitude, and be humbly appreciative of what life brings.

Jerry has spent several years designing and perfecting the concept of Managing Brand YOU, and now with the collaboration of his coauthor, Ira Blumenthal, these principles are readily accessible in book form.

He enjoys speaking publicly to large or small audiences on topics ranging from personal motivation and development to creating long-lasting strategic alliances. He has consulted with many dif-

ferent clients regarding strategic planning and long-term growth paths.

Jerry is happily married to his best friend, Virginia, and they reside in Atlanta. Their daughter, Abigail, is currently a college student. All three of them volunteer at the Atlanta Ronald McDonald House where Jerry is a member of the Board of Directors.

Jerry can be reached through his website at www.jerryswilson.com.

IRA BLUMENTHAL

Respected as a modern day business *"Renaissance Man,"* Ira Blumenthal wears many hats. He is the founder and president of CO-OPPORTUNITIES, Inc., an Atlanta-based consulting company that has counseled world class clients such as Coca-Cola, Nestle, Trump Entertainment, McDonald's, Harrah's, Delta Airlines, Exxon, Wal*Mart, Marriott, and others in areas related to branding, strategic alliances, business development, and change management. He is also the President of The Captain Planet Foundation, a not-for-profit public charity that funds educational and inspirational programs for children so that they can become great stewards of the planet and live eco-friendly lives. Ira is also the inaugural Executive-In-Residence at Georgia State University's Cecil Day School of Hospitality. Above and beyond these roles, Ira is also a much-in-demand public speaker who delivers over fifty keynote speeches annually, and has addressed audiences on four continents. He has served as the speaker "opener" for leaders such as President George Bush (Sr.), General Colin Powell, Bob Dole, Lech Walesa, Henry Kissinger, and others. Ira has been featured and quoted in media sources such as the *Wall Street Journal*,

BrandWeek magazine, *USA Today*, *Entrepreneur* magazine, and CNN. He has published over 100 articles on business development, and is the author of *Ready, Blame, Fire!* a book that focuses on the myths and misses in marketing. He is the recipient of the Educational Foundation's highest honor for his contributions to ". . . spirited, innovative business education . . . ," as well as the George Washington Honor Medal for Literary Excellence presented by the Freedoms Foundation. Ira has been a visiting university instructor at the University of Notre Dame and Michigan State University. On a personal note, Ira is on civic boards, is a children's advocate, a tireless community activist, and a long-time youth travel team baseball coach with many championships to his credit. In his own youth, Ira was a standout athlete and served as an NCAA football and lacrosse coach, as well as player-coach of the USA World Cup Mens Masters Lacrosse Team. Originally from New York, Ira lives in Atlanta with his redhead wife, Missouri bride, Kim. He is the father of two daughters, three sons, and has a grandson.

Ira can be reached through his website: www.IraSpeak.com.